There I Find Love

Strawberry Sands Book Three

Jessie Gussman

Published By: Jessie Gussman

Contents

Acknowledgements

Cover art by Kim Killion of The Killion Group

Editing by Heather Hayden

Narration by Jay Dyess

Author Services by CE Author Assistant

Listen to the unabridged audio for FREE performed by Jay Dyess on the Say with Jay channel on YouTube. Get early access to all of Jay's recordings and listen to Jessie's books before they're available to the general public, plus get daily Bible readings by Jay and bonus scenes by becoming a Say with Jay channel member .

Chapter 1

Alexander Hudson flipped a pen through his fingers while staring out the floor-to-ceiling windows in his corner office overlooking Lake Michigan.

Chicago was his hometown, although he certainly hadn't been born on this side of it.

In fact, in order to get here, he'd had to do the opposite of everything every person who knew him expected him to do in life.

Succeed, for one.

He sighed and turned his face away from the view and walked to his desk. He picked up the water that sat there, took a swig, then walked back to the window, the pen never stopping its movement around his fingers.

Normally, Saturday mornings were his favorite morning to work. There was little noise in the offices, he was seldom bothered, the phone didn't ring much, and he and his administrative assistant, Clara, had all the time and privacy in the world to lose themselves in their work.

Except today, Clara wasn't here.

Twisting on his foot, he strode back to the desk, then turned and started back to the window without taking a drink.

She had wanted to go home.

Like Chicago wasn't her home. She belonged here. Belonged in the office with him, helping him, taking his notes and instructions, looking up information, making coffee, grabbing lunch, sending emails, and...giving a little sunshine to his soul.

He pursed his lips. Turning abruptly, he strode to the other wall, past the large windows and the beautiful view. Barely seeing it. He made a lap around his office, large and luxurious, the kind of office he could only dream about as he ascended the ladder, coming from the slums of the city one small step at a time. Through hard work, determination, and perseverance, he'd earned this corner office. And he'd worked hard to keep it.

But somehow, the success that he'd always thought would feel so good didn't really feel like success. He didn't have the satisfaction, didn't feel happy...except when he was around Clara.

She had a smile and way about her that was friendly and cheerful, even on his grumpiest days.

It was far, far different than anything he'd experienced growing up. He really didn't know anyone else like her. She trusted way too easily, which he scoffed at, warned her about, and finally had tried to protect her from. From herself.

She was so different from everyone else he knew. Most people were sarcastic and self-focused. People who would say if someone was too cheerful or too happy or too eager to please, they had self-esteem issues that needed to be worked on.

He'd spent enough time in therapy to know that.

But sometimes, he wondered exactly what his therapist knew. After all, from the little bit that he talked to her about personal issues, she didn't seem to have a very happy life herself.

That had made him dig deeper, and eventually he quit going. She'd been divorced twice, had been currently fighting over custody of her two children—not fighting for custody, fighting to not have it—and had been suicidal.

He considered himself a little bit crazy to be thinking that he could go to someone like that and get life advice for himself.

He wanted life advice from someone like Clara. Someone who seemed happy and cheerful, someone other people enjoyed being around and who seemed content and at peace with her life.

His entire life, he was looking for that contentment and peace. He hadn't found it yet.

That wasn't his problem this morning though.

His problem was he suspected that Clara wanted to quit.

It was something he'd heard as he was passing the water cooler the previous week. Normally, he didn't walk around without reading something. After all, there was no point in wasting any time. So normally he had his head down and didn't pay attention to the people around him. But when he heard Clara's name, his attention had been diverted. It was just a snippet of information. But the line that he'd heard, "Clara is out of here soon," had made his heart drop like a rock and his hands tremble.

There wasn't anyone else who worked in the office named Clara. Not that he knew of anyway. But just in case, he checked.

Clara Landry, his administrative assistant, was the only Clara in the company.

And apparently, she was quitting.

Just a few weeks ago, he had asked her to move to the Cities with him. He was starting a new office there, and it would take six months to a year to get things up and running. He didn't want to do it without her. Actually, he really didn't want to do much of anything without her. Funny how she'd come to be indispensable to him.

He hated that. That was why he didn't get close to people. Because they never stayed. He'd been abandoned by way too many people who were never supposed to leave him, way too many times in his life, and he should know better than to get complacent now.

The trouble was, he didn't know what to do. He could just let her go, but there was something in him that didn't want to do that.

He knew he couldn't hold her. No one could hold another person, or change them, as much as they might like to. He'd learned that with his parents.

But Clara. She was different.

He pressed his lips together as he stared out, unseeing, at the blue-on-blue beauty of Lake Michigan and the wide expanse of the sky. There had to be a way. He could offer her more money. Of course. But he'd offered her more to move to the Cities. A lot more. He already paid her more than any administrative assistant that he knew was making anywhere. It couldn't be the money.

Was it him?

People often said he was a difficult man to work for. He supposed that was true. He held others to the same high standard that he held himself to. But he didn't ask anyone to do anything that he wouldn't do himself.

Had he been unkind to her?

He supposed he'd taken advantage of her. He felt her large compensation package would keep her and hadn't considered that it might take more.

But then again, maybe what he'd overheard was just office gossip.

He liked that idea. But there was only one way to find out. He wasn't the kind of man to sit around. He pulled his phone out of his pocket and dialed Clara's personal cell phone number. It was the only number he had for her.

He tapped his fingers on his desk as he waited for her to answer.

"Hello?"

"Are you coming out to the Cities?" He probably should have tried to do some small talk, but he'd never learned how. He always cut to the chase.

"I thought I had until the middle of July to decide." Did she sound annoyed? Scared? And what was going on in the background? It sounded like she was in the middle of some kind of concert or something.

"I've changed my mind." He could hardly tell her he was scared to death of trying to do life without her in it. That she was the only bit of sunshine his soul ever saw. That she made him feel like he was almost human. He couldn't lose her, and her words sounded far too much like she was planning on telling him no and just needed more time to get enough nerve to do so.

He made a spur-of-the-moment decision. The kind of decision his gut was famous for, the kind that had landed him multimillion dollar accounts, because he wasn't afraid to lay himself out when he believed the winds were turning in his favor.

"I've decided we're both going to work remotely from that little town you want to stay in. What's it called? Strawberry Pie Place or something?"

"Strawberry Sands. It's a lakeside town." She paused, and his heart thumped hard. Was she going to say no? "You're moving here?"

He hadn't considered going quite that far. But in a snap, his mind was made up. That would work. That would absolutely work.

"Yes." He said the word with confidence. This would give her what she wanted—to live near her family—and it would give him what he wanted, too: Clara. Working for him.

His mind immediately turned the questions into answers and a to-do list. He rattled it off. "I can work remotely as long as they have good internet, and I will make sure they do. I'll have everything set up in two weeks. Send me the directions. I'll drive in today, and we'll have a meeting to hash everything out. I want the best place to set up shop. The staff you'll need to hire. Office equipment you'll need to purchase and job duties. We'll end up traveling a lot together, as we'll need to go to the Cities at least once per month for in-person meetings."

"Today?"

"Yes."

"It's Saturday."

Shoot. He'd totally forgotten. Man, she probably thought he was some kind of loser that he was in his office at this hour on a Saturday morning. Although she knew him from working with him for years and knew he worked Saturdays almost every week.

She just didn't realize what the thought of her leaving had done to him. He thought of making up some kind of excuse that he'd had a date, but she bailed, but one of the things he'd sworn he'd never do was lie. His parents had lied to him enough. He valued the truth and tried to live it. He especially wanted to do that with Clara.

"You're right. I'll buy you dinner. There is someplace to eat there, right? Then we'll talk."

"Um... I have a stand...at the...Strawberry Festival."

It was a slap in the face to be confronted with the fact that she had a life outside of his. For some reason, that made him feel left out and...lonely. That she had friends and fun and family, and he...was at his office on a Saturday morning trying to figure out how to keep his administrative assistant from quitting because she was the closest thing he had to a friend.

"Fine. We'll meet there. Text me directions."

He slid his phone off before she could turn him down. Hopefully, she would come through with directions for him. If she didn't... He picked up his phone and Googled "Strawberry Festival in Strawberry Sands." He could find her himself.

Chapter 2

"I wasn't expecting this many people," Kristen said as she popped the rest of the strawberry tart into her mouth.

"I wasn't either. I admit I'm glad that there is a huge crowd, and I can't believe the number of paintings I sold." Clara held up the tart she had in her fingers. "Although in a way, I wish there were less people, because Griff sold out of these."

"That's sad," Kristin agreed, and they exchanged dreary looks.

But then Clara's face brightened. "But we live in Strawberry Sands, and so does Griff. Surely he'll be making these for the diner at some point."

"I'm sure he will be. But I already go to the diner way more than I should, and I've already gained ten pounds this summer. I wish he could make something that wasn't delicious."

"He does seem to have a knack for coming up with things that I feel like I can't get enough of. Do you think he has some kind of secret ingredient?" Clara wasn't really into conspiracy theories, but she was feeling light and happy and excited. Although, the conspiracy theory idea was totally to get her mind off the fact that her boss was on his way to Strawberry Sands.

"It's possible. MSG is a standard ingredient in Chinese food, and everybody knows how addicting that is."

They laughed together as they stood on the sidewalk beside Clara's painting booth.

There were at least five people perusing the artwork she had left, and she could hardly believe that she had sold more than thirty paintings that day.

"The funny thing is," she lowered her voice, glancing at the casual customers, "I almost didn't do this at all. It's only because Jubilee talked me into it. And even then, I was just going to bring a few paintings and prepare to be bored all day."

Kristin laughed. "I think Strawberry Sands is growing. I've heard rumors about land values, and I think this is case in point. We didn't even advertise it that much."

"Jubilee told me that she didn't even know who was going to be performing until this week."

"I know! What town does their festivals like that? And yet, people came."

It was rare that Kristin managed to have a few moments away from her gram. Kristen was running what was essentially an assisted living facility since her gram and her gram's two friends moved in.

Clara had always enjoyed Kristin's sense of humor and her down-to-earth personality. And while Clara spent a lot of time in Chicago for her job, she still cherished the time she spent with her childhood friend.

"I've heard Luke complaining that Miss Heather is trying to get you two together." Maybe she shouldn't have brought it up, but she always told her brother to stuff it and try to imagine himself in Kristin's shoes, but it never really worked.

"You know, even before my grandma came, Luke and I never really got along."

"It didn't have anything to do with that time you both almost got lost on the lake in the sailboat?"

"Maybe. Although, I forgave him for that a long time ago."

"You forgave him?" Clara couldn't help saying incredulously.

Kristin nodded with innocence.

"You mean it was his fault?" Clara said, clarifying.

"Yeah. Why? Does he blame me?" Kristin said, and Clara wasn't sure whether she was angry or thought it was funny.

"He does. I never even thought to ask if it was something he had done."

"Why that..." Kristin's words trailed off as a lady walked up to Clara.

"How much for this one? I don't see a tag on it."

Clara gave Kristin a look, and her friend nodded, understanding she needed to get back to her customers. Kristen gave a little wave as Clara turned to the lady, looking at the painting.

"That one is fifty dollars," she said with confidence. She had no idea. But if it didn't have a tag, she was going to make something up. After all, that's what she did when she priced them out last night. It wasn't like it was rocket science. She just put prices on them and then ended up being shocked all day as people actually paid what she asked.

"All right. I'll take this one and the one that my husband's holding over there."

"All right. Come on over here and you can pay. Cash or card?"

She walked to the little table she had set up with her credit card machine on the top and a cash register beside it. She was grateful she had had the foresight and the knowledge to get the credit card machine, since that's how most people had paid.

"If you'd like me to, I can wrap these up for you," she offered as she handed the lady her card and receipt.

"Our car is parked right down the road. I'll have my husband carry them straight there. Thanks anyway," the lady said. "Do you have a shop somewhere?" she asked as Clara started to turn away.

"I—"

"Miss Landry. I found you."

Her mouth clamped closed. She knew that voice. Would recognize it anywhere. Heard it quite often in her dreams actually.

It was her boss, Alexander Hudson.

"Mr. Hudson. I... I thought you would be a little later."

"We didn't set a time, and you know I believe in being early."

She nodded.

The lady with whom she had been talking had looked between the two of them a couple of times before she opened her mouth and asked the question that made Clara want to sink through the floor. "I'm sorry. Did you say you had a shop somewhere?"

"No. She doesn't. She is my administrative assistant and an excellent one at that. Excuse us."

Alexander gave the woman a look that had dismissed entire rooms of high-powered businesspeople. The poor lady didn't have a chance but scurried away, grabbing her husband in the process.

Clara wasn't even tempted to smile. And she still had the feeling that if the ground opened up and swallowed her whole, it would be a blessing.

"Let's go somewhere we can talk," Alexander said, not even looking to make sure the woman walked off.

"I can't leave. This is my stand, and I'm responsible for it."

"Call whoever's artwork this is and have them come and man their own stand. You're busy."

He didn't realize it was hers. Of course not. She certainly never mentioned her artwork to him. Why would he care?

Chapter 3

"Excuse me, miss?" Clara felt a tug on her sleeve. "Can you tell me how much this is?"

Another one? She would have sworn she put prices on all of her paintings.

"It's one thousand dollars," Alexander said. "Show special. Tomorrow, it goes up to ten thousand."

The woman's eyes got big, and Clara opened her mouth to say it was no such thing before the lady said, "I've fallen in love with it. I have to have it. It's the perfect picture to go over the mantel of my fireplace at home. I grew up along the shores of the Great Lakes, but I live in Kentucky now, and this picture will take me home every time I see it."

Clara's mouth snapped closed. The woman talked like she was going to actually pay that much for it.

"Do you want anything else?" Alexander said, his voice brimming with confidence.

Clara figured she should probably step in. A thousand dollars for that picture was crazy. But she was too bemused as Alexander stepped to the small desk, took the credit card from the lady, and expertly ran it like he did that all the time.

As his administrative assistant, Clara wasn't even sure he knew how to use a coffeepot.

By the time the lady left, she was convinced she had gotten the biggest bargain in the world, and Clara still hadn't found her voice.

"So these are yours?" Alexander said, and it was probably a question, but it sounded more like a statement.

"Um, yes?" Which was a question that should have been a statement.

"How much for everything that's left?"

A thousand dollars was more than she had been expecting to make for the entire day, and he just sold one picture for that.

Maybe two could play this game.

"Ten thousand dollars." Her voice sounded cool and confident.

Was that humor in his dark brown eyes? Maybe a brow raised. But there was no other indication that he was amused or surprised.

"I'll give you fifty thousand dollars for everything. You can run my card, and you know I'm good for it. Then let's get this stand shut down so we can go somewhere and talk business."

His card had just touched her fingers. She closed her hand around it but didn't move.

"This is my business."

She didn't know where those words came from. She didn't typically talk back to him at all. Whatever he said went. Of course, typically when they interacted, he was the boss and she was his assistant. However, currently, she was the artist and he was a patron. Still, the dynamic didn't feel right.

And to her consternation, her fingers trembled.

Not because she was scared, because that was her body's reaction any time she was around Alexander. He intrigued her, inspired her, intimidated her, and made her knees weak. He infiltrated her dreams and made her sigh.

He was also bossy, controlling, and she almost wanted to say ruthless. Although, she knew he had a soft side. She also knew he had a difficult past, although she didn't know the details. No one seemed to. But speculation had run rampant, from him being stolen as a child, forced to work as a sex slave and worse.

Clara figured most of those were grossly exaggerated, but they didn't quell her curiosity.

Alexander's lips turned up just a little. His look was almost chilling. "That's what we're going to talk about."

She tried to swallow, but her throat was too dry. Instead, she lifted her chin and finished pulling the card from his fingers.

Fifty thousand dollars was a tiny amount of money to Alexander. A little bit of nothing. But it was six months' salary to her. And he had just dropped it without blinking on her paintings.

Was she crazy to be leaving a company headed by a man like that?

At least he'd given her good seed money if she decided to start a new business. But she wasn't fool enough to think that it would be enough to live on for the rest of her life. Could she make a living at this?

Maybe she should continue to work for Alexander and have her shop open in the evenings and on weekends.

She considered that as she ran his card.

Rather than standing in front of her watching her, he had started to walk around the shop, his hands behind his back.

She half expected him to tell the current browsers of the shop that it was closed and the paintings were no longer for sale, but she didn't hear a word.

Instead, he stopped at the back wall, where she'd hung ten large paintings on the canvas that lined the entire back of her tent.

He stood in front of one in particular, one she had painted using her brothers' herd of horses for inspiration.

Ranger, her favorite horse from childhood, stood in the center. She'd lost Ranger almost five years ago, and she'd cried for days. She'd actually taken three days of work off and come home to help her brothers and family bury him. He'd been the horse that she'd grown up with, learned to ride on, and had spent hours on the beach with. In the painting, he was not arthritic and sick anymore, but he had his head lifted proudly, his mane flowing in the breeze along with his tail. Several of the other horses from her childhood were there, along with Cal, their dog.

That whole painting was a time capsule of her idyllic childhood. Somehow, her mom had managed to shield her from most of the care and worries, and she hadn't even really been affected too much when her dad had left. Her mom had acted like everything was just fine, and if her mom cried or even had bad days, Clara had never been aware of it. She just had her horses and her dog and the lake and sun and snow and wind, and thinking about it now made her feel a deep, happy contentment at her life and the family and friends that had surrounded her all through her growing-up years.

That picture brought it all to light. The little girl in it was holding hands with a taller, older boy. She imagined the little girl to be herself and the older boy to be her brother Matt. Her mother was off in the distance, and her sisters and brothers played around them. It was a carefree, happy picture with horses and wind and dogs and fun and smiles. So much like her childhood.

By the time she was done running his card, Alexander was still standing in front of it. She walked back to him. "Here's your receipt and your card back."

He took it from her, his fingers brushing hers, sending something warm and sweet up her arm, but his eyes never left the painting in front of him. "Why didn't I know you could paint?"

"I guess you never asked." She had never bothered to tell him. She could have said that too. But she hadn't because she didn't think he'd be interested. They didn't talk about personal things. They talked about business, because that's what Alexander always focused on.

"And you couldn't just volunteer the information?" He finally turned to look at her, his eyes dark and hooded, his face impassive, although she got the feeling that he was angry.

"Between dictating emails, fetching your coffee, and retrieving information for your business?" She didn't know where her bravery came from. She didn't typically talk to him about anything other than work. Typically, it was a "yes, sir" or "no, sir" type of communication.

She tried to be pleasant, smiling when she could, and she always got along well with the staff. She might have to work in Chicago, but she wasn't leaving her small-town roots behind. The roots that dictated she was friendly to everyone, because they were probably someone who, if she didn't know them, knew her parents, or her siblings, or both.

That wasn't true in the big city, but a workplace could feel like family, if enough people made the effort to have it that way. Plus, she didn't want to work somewhere where she wasn't comfortable. Where she didn't feel like the environment was friendly and uplifting.

She hated the cutthroat feeling of many businesses.

"Is it that bad?" he finally murmured, his face relaxing just a bit, his head tilted, as though he were truly interested in her answer.

She would bet he didn't even know her first name. He called her Miss Landry and didn't seem to realize that she was human.

But he was waiting for her answer.

"No." That was not a lie. Working with him was not bad. He was a very generous boss, and he never asked her to work hours that he didn't. He might ask her to do jobs that he didn't do, but that was because he was busy doing something else. Things she couldn't do.

"But?" The word was spoken softly, and if she didn't know him, she might have thought there was some insecurity in his voice.

"I love this! I have to have it!" a lady exclaimed from the other side of the tent.

She held a watercolor Clara had done with fall colors, showing the changing leaves, and somehow, she could almost feel the breeze and smell the spicy fall scent. Could feel summer slipping away, winter closing in fast. Hot chocolate, deep snows, cozy fireplaces, and all that winter entailed seemed to be a promise hovering just on the horizon. Looking at that picture always made her smile.

"I'm sorry. But all the paintings in this tent have been sold." Alexander didn't hesitate with his response.

The woman's face fell. "Can I get a copy?" she asked quickly as Alexander strode to the side of the tent, pulling the canvas closed.

"I'll consider it. Leave your name and number on the table. I'll let you know."

His answers were so quick, they left Clara blinking. She needed time to think and process. To get over the surprise that anyone would pay for her art.

But it was encouraging too, as the lady came over with a pen, digging in her purse for a scrap of paper to leave her information on.

"If you give it to me, I can type it into my phone," Clara offered.

The lady gave a relieved smile and rattled off her name, address, and phone number. "Please don't forget about me. There's just something so compelling about that picture. I... I feel like I could step into it."

Clara smiled. That was exactly what she wanted. She wanted people to feel, not just see.

"I know what you mean," Alexander murmured softly.

Clara's head jerked toward him, but his back was toward her, and all she could see was the lady looking at him with her brows lifted.

Something seemed to pass between them, some unspoken communication, and the lady nodded, smiling with an almost motherly smile before she turned and walked out of the tent.

Alexander didn't move for a moment before he walked over, pulling the tent flaps closed and tying them together. "What else do you have to do to close up?"

So commanding. So confident. So determined that she was going to leave with him.

Of course, she'd taken his fifty thousand pretty easily, and all of the merchandise in the tent was his. So why shouldn't she leave? She just...felt a little railroaded.

"Nothing. Other than maybe lock the cash register. And I suppose I should take my credit card machine with me."

"Since that's such a hot item?" he asked, and she had to look at him twice, because she thought he might have been joking. But in the seven years that she'd been working with him, she'd never caught him joking, not one time.

"I don't know. I just... I guess if someone figured out my password, they could get into it."

"Your password should be something that people can't figure out." He paused, looking at her hard. "It's your birthday, isn't it?"

"No?" she said, although it was. She huffed out a little laugh. "Yes. It's my birthday. Why? That's pretty hard for people to guess, isn't it?"

His lips pulled back, and they pressed together hard. His look said he guessed it on the first try.

She raised her brows. "You don't know when my birthday is."

His lips pursed, and his eyes narrowed. "I could find out if I wanted to."

A little part of her withered. She had hoped that maybe he knew. If he did, maybe this attraction she felt wasn't all one-sided. But the fact that he didn't...yeah. He didn't care.

But that was not news to her, and she was not going to allow it to get her down.

"Well, then, I'm safe. Because it might be my birthday, but if the person who's trying to steal my information doesn't know what it is, it doesn't matter." She gave him a triumphant grin, pulling out her happy spirit and her desire to be friends with everyone. If not friends, at least on good terms. She hated it when relationships weren't well received.

"You're not safe. Because you didn't hear me. I can find out when your birthday is."

"But you're not going to take the time to do that. Not for the art in this tent, painted by an unknown and unrecognized artist, in the middle of a small town in the middle of nowhere. There's nothing worth stealing."

"I just paid fifty thousand dollars for the merchandise inside this tent. To most people, that's not nothing."

She couldn't argue with that.

Chapter 4

Alexander stood in the tent, projecting an air of confidence that he really didn't feel. Clara had shocked him more than a little with her artwork. He wasn't an expert in it, but he'd gone to his share of art shows, had artists as friends, and even had extensive artwork hanging in both his condo and his residence outside of Chicago.

He didn't think Clara's art would ever hang in a gallery in New York City, but it was definitely work that pulled at his emotions, feelings, made him long for something he didn't have and didn't even realize he wanted until he looked at her pictures.

Those were feelings that made him uncomfortable but that he could also recognize in others who were looking at her work.

She had a gift. Maybe not a gift of classic art, but a gift of reaching people through her painting.

He was happy for her in a way. But that feeling was overshadowed by fear. Fear that he actually would lose her. No wonder she wanted to quit. She probably wanted to open her own art gallery and do what she was born to do, which was paint.

He put that thought aside. He could offer her more money. Offer her less hours. And if he were in town working, she could paint on the job even. They would figure something out. He was an expert at figuring things out and making them work. That's how he had become successful at everything he had done.

"Is there someplace to eat around here?" he asked, watching her fingers as they fiddled with her purse that sat on the desk in front of her.

"Well, there are lots of food vendors up and down the street right now. But the best place to eat is probably the diner. Griff has been making some really great strawberry tarts, although there's so many people that he sold out of those."

He wasn't sure who this Griff person was, but he didn't like that Clara spoke about him with such admiration.

Still, he had a philosophy that it was better to face a person's adversaries than run from them, so he said, "All right. Let's head to the diner. You have to be hungry."

He wasn't used to thinking about people other than himself, but to his eyes, Clara looked exhausted, with circles under her eyes and possibly her fingers were trembling a little as well.

She should probably eat, and then she should probably go to bed. He would have to make sure it happened.

"I am. I haven't eaten anything but two strawberry tarts all day."

No wonder she looked exhausted and was shaking.

"How far is it? Should I figure out how to get my car down here so we can drive?" They had the street blocked off, and he had parked in a sandlot behind a big building that looked like it was being used as a dog kennel.

"It's less than a block. They're actually thinking about moving the diner down to the end of the street so that they can use the patio as a dining area and people can sit and eat and see the horses and the lake." She smiled, a soft, wistful smile. One that made him wish she was smiling for him. "It's so pretty. But there's a lot of work that needs to be done to it. And I don't think Chi has been overly blessed with money."

He narrowed his eyes just a bit. Clara, more than anyone, knew that he could afford to help anyone he chose. Although, he typically invested his money in things he thought were going to be profitable for him. Not in a rinky-dink diner in some tiny town that probably wasn't going to amount to anything. Although, he was shrewd enough in business to understand that property values could possibly go up considering that Strawberry Sands was located along the lake and not too terribly far from Chicago. People were willing to drive to "get away from it all," and the folks here could take advantage of that, if they offered the right mix of tourist attractions.

His mind started to spin with the possibilities, but he tried to shut it down.

He wanted to focus on Clara right now. Focus on keeping her as his administrative assistant, focus on getting around this idea that she might want to try to use her painting to make her way in the world and she would no longer need her job with him.

How could he make her stay?

He pulled the flap back, and she ducked outside. The crowd was thick, with people walking up and down the sidewalk, laughing and smiling while some of them hummed along with the music.

"Sounds like a local band," he said, not meaning to sound snobby, but the music wasn't the type of music that he was used to listening to in Chicago. It wasn't the type that anyone would hire to play on the street there.

"It is. Jubilee found them not too far from here, and thankfully they weren't booked. She did it on a spur of the moment."

She didn't sound upset. Or even resentful. That was one of the things he had come to admire about her, if he was putting anything into words, which he usually didn't. Clara didn't complain about other people. Not about them not doing their job, not about them making more work for her when they messed up. She just took it the way it came and dealt with it that way.

Not blaming, not complaining, just getting things done. That was part of what made her a great administrative assistant. She didn't waste time on things she couldn't control, she just took what she had and did the best with it.

They started walking up the sidewalk, passing a tent that held various signs that looked like they were hand-painted, another one that had interesting pieces of driftwood, and yet another that was filled with photographs of the lake.

"I set up a showing tomorrow at eleven for a house on the bluffs overlooking the lake. It should work as a residence and an office. I'd like for you to come along with me so I can make sure that you have everything you need."

"I'm sorry. I can't."

"What?" He stumbled, caught himself, and continued to walk. But his mind was whirling. Why couldn't she?

"I'm sorry. I said I can't. If you change it to any time after twelve thirty, I'll be sure to be there. But I'll be in church at eleven."

Of course. It was a small town. He forgot. People still went to church.

Back a long time ago, he'd ridden the bus to church. He supposed some of those lessons still stuck. Although he hadn't been there in a long time.

Clara glanced over at him, and her look seemed uncertain. She opened her mouth, closed it again, and he almost laughed when she opened it once more.

He was on the verge of telling her to just say whatever it was she wanted to say, when she spoke. "You can come with me if you want. If you're going to be here."

She'd just invited him to church. He was here, trying to keep her from quitting on him, and he got an invitation...to church.

Was that a good thing or a bad thing? All of his business experience combined did not compute to let him know how he should take that invitation.

Still, his gut told him that if it was time that he wanted with Clara, he would be a fool to turn down anything she suggested.

"All right. I'll pick you up. Where and when?"

"Where are you staying?"

There were no hotels in town, so he'd booked the closest he could. "Blueberry Beach." He'd actually booked it himself. Typically, that was a job that Clara would do for him. Whether she recognized that or not, he wasn't sure. Maybe that's what her slightly lifted brow and the turned-up corner of her lip meant.

"You could stay with my mom. She has a bed-and-breakfast. It's probably booked, but she keeps a room in the attic ready for family anytime they want to drop in. I bet you can have that."

"I wouldn't want to put your mother out. Surely there's other family staying there today. With everything that's going on." He indicated the crowds of people.

"I'll check," Clara said, pulling her phone out and sending off a quick text.

She didn't have to wait long for her reply. Her phone dinged, and she looked at it for a few seconds before she looked back up with a smile.

"It's yours if you want it."

"Okay." He'd never stayed at a bed-and-breakfast before. Typically, he had Clara book the highest quality hotel she could. Bed-and-breakfasts were just so...quaint, and they felt like something a couple would do. Not a single man on a business trip, which were the only kinds of trips he took.

She typed a few more things out on her phone, then shoved it back in her pocket. "Here's the diner," she said as they walked past a building whose entire front was glass. He could see the seats inside, and every one of them was full.

"Looks like there's going to be a wait." He didn't care. The best restaurants usually had one. Unless a person had reservations, but he was going to go out on a limb and say that the diner probably didn't take reservations.

"We can always order the food and go sit somewhere outside."

He wondered where in the world she would think to sit, but he shrugged and said, "All right."

<h1 style="text-align:center">Chapter 5</h1>

When Alexander and Clara walked into the diner, all the seats were indeed full. They hadn't made it to the cash register when a voice called out, "Clara! So good to see you! I've been hearing everyone talk about your artwork. It's the most popular thing at the festival, at least from what I hear." A small, dark-haired woman hurried out from behind the counter, her apron full of pens and notebooks and straws and stained with food, looking like she'd worn it all day. But her steps were sprightly and her smile huge.

"Really?" Clara's own smile split across her face, and it made Alexander wish that she was smiling at him, rather than at a compliment on her artwork. It made him a little jealous, if he were honest.

The two of them embraced and chatted a bit about the day and what a success it had been for both of their businesses.

Business talk was something he could understand, and he could get how a festival like this would be a boon for a small town.

The woman had barely walked away, promising to be at the cash register to take orders in just a sec, when someone else came up to talk to Clara. "Girl! What a day. I loved your paintings. I saw so many people walking around carrying one. They were such a hit!"

"Thanks so much!" Clara said, beaming as she stepped back after giving the woman a hug. "Kim, this is Mr. Hudson, my boss."

The man standing behind her holding a baby carrier watched as Kim held out her hand and Alexander shook it.

"And this is my husband, Davis," Kim said.

Alexander shook Davis's hand, and his eyes narrowed. "You look familiar."

"I believe I've heard of you. Is it Alexander Hudson?" Davis asked.

"Yeah."

"I'm Davis Grinter."

Oh, of course. That was why he looked familiar. They knew each other from having met already in Chicago. But before Alexander could say anything, Kim cut in.

"But we're not talking business today. It's a day of fun and celebration."

"Miss Landry was just talking business," Alexander said, although he wasn't sure why he was picking on her.

"She's talking about potential business. There's a difference," Kim said, smiling as though she were excited about the idea of Clara potentially starting her own business. Did the whole town know about it? And why hadn't he?

"Hey, sis," a tall man said, walking up to the group as Kim and Davis waved and walked on.

Did Clara know everyone in town? It seemed like it, because no sooner had she introduced him to the man, who actually happened to be her brother, than another woman walked up, who Clara introduced as her unofficial future sister-in-law.

They laughed over that, as though they both knew that the woman's boyfriend was going to propose.

There were so many people that Alexander had a hard time keeping the names straight. It was like being at a business conference, only no one wore name tags.

But the atmosphere was so warm and welcoming, everyone was friendly and seemed to know all about Clara and her paintings and the fact that she'd been talked into doing a booth, and he hadn't even known anything. She had a whole life on the side, and he hadn't had a clue. Not a single idea that she had a life outside the office.

It made him feel more and more left out. Even though the people were friendly and welcoming, and he tried to return in kind, he wasn't used to trusting someone without taking their measure first. Without knowing their background, and whether or not they were honest, whether they were true in their business dealings, and whether they paid their bills on time.

But this small-town stuff, this everyone knowing everyone else, knowing about their business, knowing about what was going on in their personal lives, and it seemed like Clara was related to at least half of them, was all new to him. He wasn't related to anyone.

They finally made it to the counter to order, with Clara still fielding congratulations and other comments from people who apparently knew her. One matronly older woman put her arm around Clara and squeezed, congratulating her and thanking her again for the picture that she bought.

Alexander couldn't remember the names, but it really wasn't the names that were making the impression on him. It was the way Clara was part of the community. So different than what he was used to, and so different than where he normally saw her.

"Can I take your order?" Chi, the first person who had greeted them, asked as she stood behind the register.

"I'll take your beach bakery burger deluxe, with fries, and if Griff made any more of his strawberry tarts, I'll take eight."

"I don't know if he has any—"

"A little birdie told me that you really like them, so when I made the last batch, I set these back for you." A big man, tattoos on both arms which disappeared up his sleeves, and one that wrapped around his neck, along with two hoop earrings in his left ear, and a completely bald head, looking a little bit ridiculous with the chef's apron wrapped around his waist, stepped out from the back with a plate full of little tarts wrapped in plastic wrap in one hand and his other hand out like he was expecting to get a hug from Clara.

Clara, Alex's serious and focused and completely in control secretary, squealed, jumped up with her hands clasped together and pressed against her chest, then ran, her arms out, jumping into the big man's arms and wrapping herself around him.

"Griff! You are the best!" she squealed, hugging him again.

The man looked a little embarrassed, but Alexander could tell that he was also very pleased.

"Now, don't eat these all at once. Make sure you share them with the fellow you're with. He looks like he could use some."

Clara swatted at his arm. "That's my boss. You be nice."

"He's not going to be your boss for long. I've heard that you did pretty well today, and you might be opening up your own place."

"I know I shouldn't be surprised at how fast rumors travel around here, but it surprises me every time." Clara shook her head and laughed. "I'm not going anywhere just yet. I don't want to do anything prematurely."

The man jerked his head and started to turn away.

"Thank you so much, Griff. I really, really appreciate this. These things are absolutely amazing!"

"Anything for you," Griff said as he turned and walked back into the room.

There was an odd expression on Chi's face as she watched the exchange, but mostly her eyes held deep affection for Clara as she came back, holding her prize with both hands.

"We are eating these first. They are amazing." She grinned up at him.

"I have to agree with Clara. Griff is always coming up with something strawberry, and for the festival, I should have known he was going to outdo himself. And he did," Chi said, shaking her head, with a happy smile on her face. "Business has been awesome. And we actually have been turning people away while he makes another batch in the back. I'm shocked he kept those back for you."

"I just raved about them. Kristin brought me some, and they were just so good." Clara continued to glow.

"All right, Alexander, do you know what you want?" Chi looked up at him, and he froze. He had no idea what the diner offered and even less idea of what he should order.

Clara came to his rescue. "I think you'll enjoy their chicken sandwich, grilled, with the asparagus spears if they have them. If not, the sweet potato fries with their special brown sugar dip." She turned to him. "I know that's more carbs than you like, but trust me, you will love them."

"I trust you." That was the absolute truth. He did. He always had. Normally it took him a while to warm up to people, but when he hired Clara, he felt immediately that she was someone he could totally and completely trust. That had never changed. What had changed, he wasn't sure, but he felt like his entire world had shifted, not in a big way, but in a way that would make it never the same again.

Chi put the order in, he paid for it, and they stood to the side.

"It won't take long. Griff is really good at what he does."

"You seem to know him pretty well."

"He's kinda quiet; he doesn't say a whole lot, but everyone in town knows he is head over heels for Chi, who barely knows he's alive." Clara kept her voice down, and her eyes followed Chi as she walked across the diner, waiting on tables and clearing an empty one off. "We can sit if you want to?"

The diner was crowded and loud, and everyone who came in seemed to know Clara and want to talk to her. "I'd actually rather go out. If there's someplace else close?"

He never ate outside. He hated the bugs, hated the sun, hated being hot, hated that the climate wasn't controlled down to the very degree that he wanted it to be. But all this info about Clara was new. He... He wanted her to himself.

"All right. I know the perfect place. It's my mom's backyard, and we'll be able to sit in the grass and watch the horses graze and see the lake in the distance. It's really pretty." She bit her lip. "Although there will be bugs."

"That's okay. I can handle them." Bugs were better than people who took Clara's attention off him. If someone else came up and started chatting with her, and Clara introduced him, he would be polite, but the whole time, he was chomping at the bit to get out. Not that he didn't like the people, and not that he didn't like her hometown, but he had been feeling more and more urgency to get her alone so he could talk to her. This whole idea of her painting and starting a business and leaving him was just too much. He needed to get that settled. Could hardly wait for it to happen.

Their meals hadn't been delivered when the person who was chatting with Clara sat down at the table Chi had just finished clearing off.

"You've got to try this," Clara said when they were alone, peeling back a quarter of the plastic wrap and pulling a tart out.

He wasn't much for sweets. He preferred meat, although he tried to eat a healthy mix of vegetables along with it.

But he found himself unable to tell Clara no. A little surprised. Because he didn't typically have trouble uttering the word. But come to think of it, Clara didn't typically ask him to do anything. He'd never had the opportunity to tell her no, never had to struggle with whether or not he should.

He had both of his hands shoved in his pockets, and Clara didn't wait for him to pull them out. Instead, she held it up, smiling with anticipation, and lifted it toward his mouth.

He found himself opening his mouth, allowing her to feed him, popping the entire tart into his mouth, and continuing to look at him, watching for his reaction.

He didn't have to fake it. The tart was the best thing he'd ever eaten in his life before.

And that was saying something, considering he had been to some of the finest restaurants in the entire world.

Still, he wasn't one to gush, and he did not eat quickly. He chewed it, savoring it, thinking about what he would say and how he would phrase it. He didn't want her to want to live in her hometown. He wanted her to want to be with him. He was relocating here, true, but it wasn't a permanent thing. It was only here until he had somewhere else he needed to be. And then he wanted Clara to go with him when he left.

"Well? What do you think?" Clara asked, and maybe there was just a touch of worry in her eyes. Mostly it was anticipation, as though she knew he was going to say that it was the best thing he'd ever eaten.

"Griff has a true talent. That was amazing."

Her grin got bigger, and she gave a little hop on her feet. "I knew it! I knew you would love them." She grabbed one from under the plastic and popped it into her mouth, closing her eyes and uttering a small groan as she chewed slowly, savoring as he had.

"I never knew anything could taste this good," she said as she opened her eyes after she swallowed.

"Clara! Here's your food!" Chi said from the other side of the counter.

Clara's eyes had met his, and they held, just for a couple of moments, but it was a couple of moments in time that felt like they were the only two people in the world.

When Chi called them, she broke that spell, and he wanted to take the time back so he could just look at Clara and figure things out between them.

In a business sense, he added hastily in his mind. Nothing else. Right?

Chapter 6

"Is this okay?" Clara asked as she led Alexander to the spot in her mom's backyard that she loved the most. The house was deserted. Her mom was probably still down at the festival with her grandkids, enjoying herself. While the bed-and-breakfast was most likely booked solid, the guests must have been down at the festival as well, since no one moved around the yard or house.

"This is your mom's place?" Alexander asked as he nodded, indicating the spot was just fine.

"It is. It's where I grew up. I... I'm sorry I don't have a blanket or anything to sit on." She bit her lip. She doubted that Alexander had ever sat on the ground before. He actually looked very out of place, not just in her small town, but in her mom's backyard. She was used to seeing him in the impersonal confines of his office, under fluorescent lights, wearing a suit and tie and a serious expression on his face as he stared at his laptop or tablet or phone, or whatever it was he was working on at the time. As he was always working on something.

She laughed a little at that thought. Regular people thought that folks who were millionaires, or billionaires, just sat around and counted their money all the time, but in her experience, the more successful someone was, the harder they had worked to attain it.

Unless of course they had inherited it. That was completely different. She supposed also perhaps actors and actresses, who came into a lot of money in a short amount of time, might be slightly different as well.

Successful businesspeople, in her experience, worked hard for what they got, and once they had a lot, they still continued to work. Mostly because they enjoyed it.

That was what she thought about Alexander. That he loved his work, and he lived and breathed it, not because he had a driving desire to be successful, but just because he had a driving desire to...do something. She wasn't sure.

At any rate, to her surprise, he settled down on the ground beside her.

"I guess they have everything stuck in here together," he said as he looked in the package he carried. She had their drinks, one in each hand, and she handed one to him.

"Thanks. I..." He looked around. "We just set this on the ground?"

"Yeah. I... I guess this wasn't the best idea I've ever had." She didn't mind at all. She ate on the ground all the time. One of her favorite things to do was to head down to the lake and eat a sandwich and just watch the waves roll in. She loved doing it beside the pasture where the horses grazed. Just so she could watch them. There was something so relaxing about horses and the beach that made her want to sit and stay and enjoy.

"No. It was my idea. There was a table that was cleared up in the diner, and I said I wanted to leave. I just... I don't think I've ever done this before."

She laughed a little. "That does not surprise me at all. However, the fact that you're a little unsettled does surprise me." And it made her nervous as well, although she felt like she was doing a good job of covering it.

She was more comfortable in the diner surrounded by her family and friends, with a steady stream of people coming in, people whom she knew and loved. This quiet seclusion, even though it was in the backyard of her mom's house, a place where she was familiar and loved, made her less confident. Because it was just her, and while she was comfortable in Alexander's presence, having worked for him for seven years, there was still something about him that...maybe just made her wish that she was someone she wasn't, someone who would catch his eye, and that crazy feeling she had of wanting to be more with him was attainable instead of a major pipe dream.

"Why are you laughing? Seeing me sit on the ground?"

"Well, that is something I don't think I've ever seen before," she said, refusing to wipe the grin off her face.

"I'm afraid if I set my tarts on the ground, the ants will get them," he said, holding up the tarts.

"Maybe we should eat those first." Why not? Was it so terrible to eat dessert first?

"What's that saying? The one about life is short, so eat dessert first?"

"I'm surprised you know that one."

"I must have seen it fifteen times today as we walked along the sidewalk, looking at the different shops."

"Oh." That explained it. Alexander was an extremely intelligent person. She'd figured out that much about him after spending five minutes with him when she was first hired.

He didn't forget much, and he noticed everything.

Except her birthday. She almost rolled her eyes at that. She hadn't expected him to know, but there'd been a part of her that had been a little disappointed.

Without saying anything more, he set the bag of food from the diner aside and peeled back the plastic that covered the tarts. "I don't think I needed that saying to convince me that these things are good enough that we should definitely eat them first. I would be upset if ants got even one bite."

She grinned a little, looking up at him, wondering if he was being sincere, or if he was making fun of her somehow.

He was not the kind of person who talked badly about people. In the seven years that she worked with him, she barely heard him say an unkind word, unless it was definitely deserved and more along the lines of not wanting to work with someone again, for the sake of the company, not a personal attack.

But this... This seemed a little fanciful for her version of Alexander.

"I think the small town is rubbing off on you," she said, a little uncertainly as she reached over to get a tart.

"No." He moved the plate some so her fingers grasped at air. "I don't think that's how it's done. At least, that's not how you did it earlier."

Her brows drew down, and she looked at him, confused.

He lifted his brows, almost as though challenging her, and then he picked up a tart. Surely he wasn't going to eat the entire plate himself?

She was going to protest about that. After she got over her surprise.

But he didn't feed himself the tart. Rather, his hand moved toward her. She almost reached for it, but she realized after a second or two what he was actually doing. He was going to feed her. The way she had fed him in the diner. Only she had done it because... She wasn't sure. If she remembered correctly, he had his hands in his pockets, and she just hadn't waited for him to get them out to reach for the tart. She'd been excited, wanted him to taste it immediately. It hadn't been anything she planned.

But the tart reached her lips, and she opened her mouth, allowing him to place it inside.

Her stomach twisted, and her breathing seemed to spin. Unable to figure out what exactly was going on. It was so unlike Alexander, who was never anything but completely professional.

"Is it still the best thing you've ever eaten, Clara?" he asked, and somehow the words sounded...romantic.

She had to admit, she wasn't tasting the tart. There were too many other things she was trying to figure out. Too many things were happening inside of her. Her chest felt wobbly, her stomach crazy, and her brain mush.

And he knew her first name. She couldn't remember him ever calling her anything but Miss Landry up until that point.

It was the way he treated all of his business associates, with old-fashioned manners and charm. It was part of his...brand. Just him being a businessman.

"It's very good," she said, and she swallowed the last of it, knowing that what she said was true, even if she hadn't tasted it.

"Aren't you forgetting something?" he asked.

"I am?" she asked, surprised.

"My name."

She stared at him. His name?

Maybe because he called her Clara, he expected her to return the favor?

It was the only thing her brain, in its weakened state, could figure.

"Alexander. It was very good, Alexander."

He smiled a little, and she felt that she had done the right thing.

Still, she couldn't help but feel that everything was surreal. Her boss was sitting in her mom's backyard, on the ground, wanting her to call him by his first name. Calling her by hers, and feeding her tarts. What in the world was going on?

It was all a little too much. Maybe it was the stuff of dreams, but believing that dream was real was harder than she thought it would be.

Call her a coward, but she scrambled to her feet, then made herself walk slowly and sedately a few more steps toward the lake, where she stopped, ostensibly to look at the view.

"This is so pretty. My mom has the best backyard in the entire world."

"I don't know. The house we're supposed to look at tomorrow has a pretty nice view from the front yard." He shifted a little, pulling his phone out of his pocket and glancing at it. "Great. The real estate agent moved our appointment to one o'clock. That should give us enough time to go to church, maybe grab a bite to eat, and ride up the beach just a little ways, if I understand correctly."

"And you want me to go with you?" she said, hating that she sounded breathless. He was sitting in her yard, feeding her tarts, and she was going to look at a house with him. Of course, it was because he wanted her to work with him, but still. It was just...odd.

"I said I did. Do I typically say things I don't mean?"

"No. You don't." She turned around, putting a relaxed smile on her face and forcing herself to not show how disconcerted he had made her with his total departure from his norm.

"You're not prone to pacing. Is there a problem?" he asked as he lifted the plate of tarts and picked another one.

She was not going to allow him to feed her again. She wasn't sure what he was thinking, but despite the crush that she had on him for years, she wasn't the kind of girl who had a fling and particularly not the kind who had a fling with her boss.

Still, she could admire the strong fingers, the competent manner, the way he looked at home wherever he was.

"No problem. I guess... It's just odd seeing you out of the office." She could be honest. "And you're right that I fed you a tart in the diner, and I suppose you owed me, but that just feels a little bit like a breach of the professionalism that has always been between us. I... I don't want you to get the wrong idea." That she was interested in anything other than a serious, long-term relationship. Which, to her knowledge, Alexander did not do.

She had been the one who had hired women, from a reputable agency, of course, for him to escort to various functions. Not every time. Several times, he'd taken famous actresses, and once he'd taken the daughter of a senator. But it typically wasn't the same woman twice, and never twice in a row.

"I'm sorry."

He sounded contrite. Maybe a little surprised. But he didn't elaborate. Thankfully, because she really didn't want him to. She didn't want him to say that that wasn't what he was doing at all. That he wasn't pushing her or attracted to her in any way, just trying to be more relaxed because of the small-town atmosphere and the fact that they were outside of the normal business setting.

That she'd taken everything wrong.

She felt her cheeks heating, but she ignored that and went back over, sitting down with a little more room between them.

If he noticed, he didn't comment. He offered her the plate of tarts, and she took one.

"No. You are right. I...didn't mean to make you uncomfortable."

She didn't say anything but took the plate silently, hoping he didn't notice that her hands trembled.

She swallowed and wished they had decided to eat in the diner, because she would be enjoying this a lot more. She'd be less nervous, less...embarrassed.

"About church. If I'm staying here—you keep calling this your mom's house, but I saw the bed-and-breakfast sign in the front when we walked by, and so I assume this is her place."

"Yes. I can show you to your attic room when we're done eating."

"I appreciate it. I want to get some work done before I go to bed tonight. In the meantime, where should I pick you up?"

"I have a little cottage, right over there. That's where I stay when I'm in town." She pointed in the general direction of her one-room cottage. It was on the lot adjacent to her mom's farm and part of the original homestead which her mom owned. Her brothers had built the cottage when they were teens, and all the siblings together had added a well and septic.

There was no kitchen, just a bed and a little desk. She bummed the internet from her mom's house and used the space heater in the winter for heat.

It wasn't much of anything, but it was a place to land when she stayed, especially during the summer when the bed-and-breakfast was booked up.

It also gave her privacy on weekends when she came home but still had to work.

She didn't mention any of that to Alexander. Although, he wasn't a dense man and probably figured out that she used it on her working weekends when she was home.

"That's perfect. I won't have to get directions to pick you up. I'll knock on your door at...ten thirty?"

"Ten forty-five might be better, and we can walk. The church is that way." She pointed toward where the church was. They couldn't see it from the yard, because of the big old oak tree and the way the land was contoured, but it was a short walk. "Maybe five minutes. I wouldn't drive unless it was raining."

"All right. I'll knock on your door at ten forty-five, unless it's raining, and then I'll... Can I drive there?" he asked, leaning around her, trying to see whether the road went toward her cottage or not.

"No. It's back off the road, and we walk to it from here. Wherever you have your car parked is probably fine. Where did they park you? In the sandlot behind the boarding kennels?" she asked, knowing that's where they usually put the overflow, and Alexander had come later in the morning.

"That's it."

"You should be fine there. I suppose you'll have to go back and grab some clothes."

"Yes. I think I can find it myself though."

"Strawberry Sands is not exactly a large town. It's not even a large small town."

"It's barely a town."

"True. But I think the smaller the town, the more close-knit everyone who lives in it is."

"I wouldn't disagree with that." He paused. "Although I have no experience."

"You grew up in Chicago?"

"Mmhmm."

He didn't seem inclined to add more, and this was the type of thing that she normally wouldn't press him on. But she wanted to know.

"It must have been a completely different world, growing up in the city."

"Yeah," he said, and his face seemed carefully blank as he put the last strawberry tart into his mouth. He chewed slowly, looking out at the lake, and seemed disinclined to answer any more questions. She wasn't sure from his expression whether it was okay for her to ask more, or whether he was politely trying to discourage her. They'd never had this problem in their relationship before. Every time they'd been together, even if they were doing lunch, which they did occasionally, it was all about business.

"Are your parents still alive?"

At first, she didn't think he was going to answer her, because he chewed slowly, swallowing, his gaze on the lake the entire time. Finally, he took a sip of his drink, set it down, and then turned to her.

"My dad died in prison. My mom is still there."

Clara's eyes got big. She had no idea. None at all. That was...shocking.

That such a great businessman, a millionaire and her boss, had a family life like that, but instantly, it made him far more relatable than he had ever been before. She didn't exactly pity him, but she felt drawn to him in a way she hadn't, even when she'd been attracted and secretly in love with him.

"Siblings?" she asked softly, care and concern in her tone.

"Just me. Fitting, since parents like mine probably shouldn't have more than one progeny."

Was he laughing? She couldn't quite tell and didn't want to laugh at an inappropriate time or over a sensitive subject.

Chapter 7

Clara decided maybe sharing something about herself would make him more comfortable.

"My dad left my mom when I was young. Mom had six kids and a farm to run. Life was hard, but I only know that because looking back, I understand what a single woman would have been facing with six kids and all that work in front of her. But at the time, it just seemed like a lot of fun. And when Dad left, that took all the stress and anger out of the house. Even though I missed him, I didn't miss tiptoeing around, hoping not to make him mad."

"Yeah. I know a little bit about that." He blew out a breath, almost as though he were pushing the thoughts aside, and reached over to grab the bag their meals were in. "Did you save room for these?"

She laughed, because usually it was saving room for dessert. "Of course. Griff is known for his desserts and for his awesome burgers."

"Wish I had known that. I would have ordered a burger instead of allowing you to order my usual chicken."

"The chicken is pretty good too. It's just the burgers that people usually come to the diner for."

"I can branch out."

Like she knew that. "I guess if it hadn't been so crowded, I wouldn't have ordered for you. And I would have taken the time to explain."

"Yeah. I was giving you a hard time. We didn't want to hold them up. Especially when that was probably the busiest day they've had all year."

"I'm sure it is. Small towns live for their festivals. Anything that brings tourists and their dollars in is a win."

"I have a little bit of trouble wrapping my head around the fact that you were painting and planning a booth while still doing your job with me. And I didn't know anything about it."

"The subject didn't naturally come up."

"You could have brought it up."

"I just tried to talk about your parents and your childhood, and you kind of gave me the cold shoulder. It makes a girl think that maybe personal issues aren't welcome in our conversations."

"My personal issues aren't welcome. Yours are."

"Is that a new rule?" she asked, pulling her burger out of the Styrofoam container, grabbing a fry, and sticking it in her mouth.

They were better when they were hot. One drawback to eating dessert first. The strawberry tarts would have been just as good if they would have eaten their regular food first.

"It's always been the rule. I'm sorry I wasn't more clear about it."

"Well, I guess I feel uncomfortable saying that my personal items are fair game while getting no access to yours. So maybe we should just stay professional. And talk about business only."

He had just taken a bite of his chicken sandwich, and he chewed it while staring at her thoughtfully. "I guess that isn't fair, is it?"

"No." She lifted her chin. She didn't usually match him head-on like this. Typically, whatever he said, she did. But this wasn't a typical lunch. It was a Saturday evening in her hometown, and they weren't in the office or doing business.

"All right. You can ask me whatever you want to. And I'll answer you. But you will agree to the same."

"All right. That sounds fair."

"Is Griff an old boyfriend?"

She blinked. She couldn't help it; her brows felt like they were touching her hairline before she laughed. "No! He's totally in love with Chi. Couldn't you tell?"

"Oh, that's right. The lady who took our orders."

"Yeah, the lady who owns the diner. She's in love with some lawyer who works in Chicago and comes up every once in a while but doesn't pay any more attention to her than he does any other available woman who will run off with him. I think so far, Chi has resisted, but I know it's been hard for her. She thinks he really likes her."

"I see. And he doesn't."

"Nope. At least none of us think so. Of course, he's a big-city guy, and you know you kinda have to overcome the prejudice of a small town when you're from the city."

"Thanks for the warning."

She put her hand over her mouth. She didn't even realize she was kind of insulting him. But she couldn't deny that it was true. "I think you find the same thing in the big city, don't you? I know I did. People laughed at me, and they still do, because I'm too friendly and nice. Because I go out of my way to help people I don't know, and that's not something that is typically done."

"It's true. You're different, and that's in a good way. I have been happy to see that over the last seven years that we've worked together, that hasn't changed. You...didn't get jaded like so many people do."

"Maybe that's because I come back here as often as I can. I don't really like it there."

"Is that why you want to quit?"

Her eyes got big. "Where did you hear I wanted to quit?" She hadn't said anything. "I mean, I haven't accepted the raise and the offer to transfer to the Cities, but...I never said I wanted to quit."

"I overheard something someone said at the water cooler. I don't think they thought I was listening, and I really wasn't. But they mentioned your name, and...that made me start."

She wasn't sure exactly what he meant by that. Those last words seemed to be important in some way, but she wasn't sure what. "Oh."

"And coming here, seeing that you had a whole tent full of paintings I didn't know about, a hobby that means a lot to you, money that you're making on the side... It surprised me. And maybe I put two and two together. Did I get four?" This last question was asked low, and there was a wobbly note to his voice that she wasn't sure what to make of.

Was he angry? Was he scared? She almost laughed out loud at the very idea. "I don't want to move to the Cities. And I already told you that I don't enjoy working in Chicago."

"And the need to move has made you think?"

"I guess. That, and the fact that my brother's girlfriend suggested that I have a booth. And then...things sold today. I wasn't expecting that. I... I know I don't want to move to the Cities. I don't want to leave my hometown and my family. It's one thing to work a couple of hours away in Chicago, it's a completely different thing to work somewhere where I couldn't go home for the weekends without a lot of hassle."

"I understand now, after seeing you today." He paused for a moment, to look out over the lake once more, watching the horses down over the hill grazing, and then looking around the backyard. "After seeing all of this. I definitely understand a little better. I... I think if this were my family and my hometown, I wouldn't want to leave it either."

She'd never seen him like this. Never seen him anything less than his most competent, put together, completely at his best.

She had to admit, she liked this side of Alexander even better than she liked the business side he showed the world. This felt more personal and somehow made her feel closer, more connected to him. Definitely it made him more relatable. Up until this point, he'd almost been someone she idolized, but now, he seemed more human. She liked it.

They sat in silence for a little bit as she finished her hamburger and opened a package of ketchup, dipping her fries in it and munching on them slowly.

He always ate faster than she did, and he was finished well before she, but he didn't move, just sat with his legs up, his arms hooked around them, staring at the lake.

"There's definitely a peacefulness here that seeps down into you," he said after a long time of silence. She could hear laughing and talking behind her for the first time, although the strains of the music had been drifting up for a while. Maybe people were starting to come home.

They would be fine out in the yard. There was nothing her mom would mind, and she wasn't in any of the guests' way, but she felt a little disappointed that her time with Alexander was over.

Maybe this is just one of those fluke things where, for just a few minutes of time, they were equals, rather than a millionaire and his hassled and harried administrative assistant.

"I can leave, but it always pulls me back," she said, putting the last fry into her mouth and brushing the salt off her fingers.

"I'm curious to see what the house looks like tomorrow. There weren't very many offerings on the market."

"I didn't even know about that one. The only thing I know for sale around here is the old schoolhouse."

He paused as he was gathering up the garbage and putting it back in the bag. "Did you go to school there?"

She knew her smile said she loved it. "I did. My siblings and I all went. They closed it down shortly after my youngest sister finished sixth grade. That's all it was, two rooms and a gym, plus some offices, housing first through third and fourth through six. The church did kindergarten." She laughed. She hadn't thought of those years in a long time. "We have some great memories there."

"You think it would make a good office/home?" He tilted his head toward her, and she hadn't realized that night had started to fall until she had to squint to see his eyes. They were already dark but now even more so when in the shadows of his face.

"Maybe? I haven't been there in forever, although we walked, so it's that close. No matter how bad it got in the winter, there was never any excuse not to go to school, since everyone walked."

"That would stink. No snow days."

"I know, right?"

"They didn't give you one, just because?"

"Sometimes we'd have a two-hour delay. And sometimes Miss Fry, she was the teacher for the younger kids, would let us spend the morning outside sledding down the hill. It was so much fun."

"Sounds like an idyllic childhood."

"It was. But here we go, talking about mine, and I still don't have any idea about yours."

He started moving again, shoving the garbage in the bag, then standing gracefully to his feet as he held out a hand for her.

She looked at it for just a moment before she took it. This was new too. They didn't typically go around helping each other. Not physical tasks.

His hands were smooth, as befitted a businessman, as her fingers slid into his, and he pulled her easily to her feet. She knew his schedule, knew he spent an hour every morning at the gym, and she doubted that he ever missed. She felt his strength just then and wondered that she had never thought about it before.

But he didn't typically wear short sleeves, and his biceps curled, and she had trouble peeling her eyes from them and looking back at his face, trying to remember what they were talking about.

"I'm asking now." She tried to focus. "What was your childhood like?"

He grinned. "Show me my room first."

She wanted to call him on that. That wasn't a part of their deal. He was supposed to tell her whatever she wanted, but to be fair, he hadn't refused. He'd just put her off. Maybe that was because he could hear the laughter which had gotten louder.

"Okay," she said.

They finished gathering up the garbage and threw it away as they entered the kitchen.

"Normally the guests come in the front door, although they have the run of the house, except Mom's room upstairs, and Jubilee and her kids' rooms. There are signs on their doors."

"All right."

"You're welcome to the back area as well. And Mom always makes breakfast for the guests which she starts serving at six o'clock. She has it buffet style, and it's usually out until ten or so. Unless she knows that all the guests have eaten."

"Good to know."

She walked ahead of him, up the stairs, as the front door opened and laughter and talking drifted up as other guests entered the house.

"I'm sorry there are two sets of stairs you have to climb," she said as they made a U-turn and walked down the hall to the turn where the second set of stairs started.

"I'll take five minutes off my time at the gym," he said easily, and she smiled to herself. Of course.

She opened the attic door and climbed the stairs. Her mom had most of the attic finished, although some of it was for storage.

"The light is right here." She flipped it on as she spoke, and he murmured, "Okay," behind her.

"When you get to the top, the bathroom is on your right, and the room that Mom always keeps ready is the next one on the right. You have a nice view of the lake from it, and the few times I stayed in it, when one of my siblings was at the cottage, I've really enjoyed the view from that high."

"I'm sure it's beautiful."

"Especially with the full moon. I... I spent more than a few hours just sitting at the window watching the way the moonlight plays on the lake. It's...enchanting. For me anyway." She didn't mean to get so personal. She had to keep reminding herself that this was her boss. The unapproachable and slightly intimidating man that she worked with. He seemed so different now.

Opening the door, she was a little embarrassed to show him how simple it was. Certainly not even as nice as a hotel room. Especially since he had to walk out of it and across the hall to go to the bathroom. It was a lot less than what he was used to.

"This is about as big as the first apartment I remember living in," he said as he stood in the doorway, looking at the simple bed with one pillow, and the small dresser that sat beside it. That was pretty much all that could fit in the room. Although there was a chair by the window. It was just a hard chair, with no cushion.

"Wasn't there a kitchen?" Clara asked, and for some reason, she kept her voice soft, as though speaking loud would make him stop sharing whatever it was he was going to share.

"I don't remember one. Mom had something she plugged into the wall, something a little bit like a Bunsen burner, that she heated water for coffee in. Or she'd use it to boil macaroni and cheese or hot dogs."

"I see."

"We didn't stay there long. We moved around a lot. Sometimes Dad was with us, sometimes it was another guy. But it seemed like Mom would go to someone else, or maybe a couple of someones, then Dad came on the scene again, and Mom would stick with him for a little bit until they couldn't stand each other anymore, and then they split again." He still stood in the doorway, but his eyes tracked over to her. "There were a lot of drugs and alcohol. I...probably won't go into that detail unless you want me to."

"No. I don't want to make you uncomfortable."

"It doesn't really make me uncomfortable. I just don't usually think about it."

"It's hard for me to imagine that you are where you are, coming from that."

"Maybe it's harder for me to imagine that I would have been where I am right now if I hadn't been there. Experiencing that, deciding I wanted to be different, that I was going to be more than someone who lived in the projects all my life. Drugs and alcohol weren't going to be my life, and they weren't going to define me."

She nodded, still feeling like she would never be able to wrap her mind around a childhood like the one that he had experienced. She and her family might have been poor growing up, but she had a solid anchor. She still did. Her mom still lived in the house she grew up in, and had no intentions of leaving. She could come back home anytime she wanted to and knew that she would be welcomed with open arms. Knew her siblings would rally around her, and the only reason she was thinking about quitting her job and trying to make a living with her painting was because she knew her siblings would catch her if she fell.

"It must have been lonely."

"At times. Sometimes my parents' friends would bring me out and laugh at me. They liked to get me drunk."

Her eyes widened. "You were a child!"

He lifted a shoulder. "On the one hand, I liked the attention. You know, positive attention. People looked at me and talked to me. But on the other hand, I figured out that I'd never seen anyone do anything smart while they were drunk. I guess that shaped me as much as anything. Maybe realizing that no one ever did anything smart while they were high, or realizing that after a person had been high, the low was worse than the high had been good, made me decide the drugs were not for me. I wanted something tangible. Something that lasted. Something that didn't need more and more in order to make you feel good."

It was the most he said, and she listened to every word. Still unable to think about a childhood like that. Figuring that he probably wasn't even telling her the worst of it. Maybe she didn't want to hear.

"In a good way, going to school seemed like an oasis. It was a good thing, because it made me want to work hard, win the approval of my teachers, and I remember more than once begging my mom to get up, even though she was hungover, and take me to school. Sometimes I walked."

"Wasn't that...dangerous?"

"I don't think so. I don't remember it being dangerous. It was just cold."

She took that to mean that he didn't always have the clothes he needed.

"I don't usually talk about that. And... I guess I don't want to hear about it at work."

"I'm a little offended that you think you might." She lifted her chin and looked at him. She had turned the lights on in the room, and the fading light from the sunset turned the entire area a glowing orange. Because of that, what he was saying felt eerie to her, when the room had always seemed, if not exactly cheerful, cozy.

"Yeah. I knew that you wouldn't do that. I'm sorry."

"You don't need to apologize. I just... I just wouldn't dream of talking to anyone about that. I see how it would be very personal to you, and it would be up to you whether or not you wanted someone to know." It struck her just then how honored she was that she actually did know. As far as she knew, no one knew anything that he just told her. It made her feel special.

"Clara! Are you up there?" a voice called from the bottom of the stairs.

"That's my mom. Come on. I'll introduce you to her."

"I'm a little intimidated. She raised six kids by herself on a farm. That couldn't have been easy," he murmured as they walked out of the room, and she shut the door behind them.

"I promise you, my mom is the least intimidating woman you'll ever meet. In fact, to know her is to love her."

Chapter 8

Lana Landry looked up the attic stairs as her daughter came down. To her surprise, there were heavier footsteps coming down behind, and a man's shadowy form appeared.

Clara had texted about using it, but Lana had forgotten. Sometimes Clara stayed just because she liked it, or sometimes one of her siblings asked to use the cottage. Either way, all of her children knew that the attic room was always open to them and their guests.

"Mom, I wanted you to meet my boss, Alexander Hudson."

Lana tried hard not to look as shocked as she felt. Clara had worked for the man for more than seven years, and Lana had heard her share of Clara talking about how demanding and intense he was. She did compliment him on his business skills and on his integrity. He was always honest and upright, according to Clara. And Clara would not lie. Clara seemed intimidated by him, almost in awe. Sometimes Lana wondered if maybe she had a crush on him, but Clara had never said.

Seven years seemed like an awful long time to have a crush on someone, and Lana had figured she'd outgrown it. However, she knew that Clara had been struggling with whether or not to accept the raise and transfer Mr. Hudson had offered her.

"Mr. Hudson, this is my mom, Lana."

"Lana, call me Alex." He looked over at Clara, and there was something in his eyes that made Lana's heart hope. Something in the way he looked at her daughter that said that there was more than met the eye to their relationship. At least on his side.

Clara's brows shot up, and Lana wouldn't have been surprised to see them bounce off the ceiling. Anytime Clara talked about her boss, it had always been "Mr. Hudson." She never called him Alexander, and if anyone called him Alex, Lana didn't know about it.

"All right... Alex."

Clara's lips turned up in what Lana felt was a forced smile. Clara was trying to look relaxed when she was anything but.

Lana stepped in, holding out her hand. "Alex. It's so nice to meet you. I hear Clara talking about you all the time. She never has anything bad to say about your integrity or your business practices, which is so impressive in today's world. From what I understand, everything you've gotten, you've gotten honestly, and you've worked hard for it. I'm impressed."

If possible, Alex almost looked embarrassed. Lana had to smother a giggle. She would guess that he wasn't used to being embarrassed, but there wasn't anything she'd said that wasn't the truth.

"Well... Thank you. I...didn't know that Clara had so many good things to say about me."

Clara didn't say unkind things about anyone, but Lana didn't mention that.

"She just loves to work, and she loves her job. But I'm sure she told you she doesn't particularly care for the city."

"She told me that today. I guess it's my fault that I never even thought to think about it before this. I feel bad about that."

"I don't hate it. I just... I like coming home." Clara smiled and looked between the two of them. She seemed to like that they were getting along okay. It made Lana wonder if maybe she was right and Clara really did have a thing for her boss.

"I'm sure you heard then that I'd asked her to move to the Cities?"

"I'm really hoping you don't take my daughter away from us. Our family is...close."

"I was getting that impression after spending a few hours with Clara today. I actually have an appointment with my realtor tomorrow to look at a property. Then Clara was telling me that the schoolhouse was for sale. I think that she and I could make that work if we were to work from here and handle both the office in the Cities and the office in Chicago. We might have to travel some, but it might be a compromise."

"You would leave Chicago? What about your family?" Lana couldn't stop herself from asking, even though she knew that modern children didn't typically stick around and hang out with their parents much.

"There isn't anyone who is going to miss me if I leave the city."

Lana wasn't under the mistaken impression that Alex wanted to talk about that anymore.

"Did you get something to eat? I have a few things set out on the sideboard for the guests who are arriving back from the festivities. Some fruit, a couple of little desserts, and that type of thing. Help yourself if you're interested. I... I assume Clara invited you to stay in the attic room tonight?" Lana said as she led the way down the hall and toward the steps.

"She said it would be okay," Alex answered.

"Of course. You're absolutely welcome. Anytime. A friend of Clara's is a friend of mine."

"He's my boss, Mom. Not my—"

"Aren't we friends?" Alex's voice was low, and maybe he had meant it only for Clara's ears. But Lana was old, and her hearing was not as good as it used to be, but with her hearing aids, she picked up a lot of things that she didn't used to.

"I... I guess we are," Clara said softly. So softly Lana almost didn't hear. But she could tell that Clara was breathless. And Lana guessed it wasn't from descending the stairs.

"All right. You two can help yourselves. If you don't mind, I'm going to go see to our guests," Lana said, excusing herself with a little smile. She wasn't sure exactly what was happening, but she would say that the relationship was evolving in a way that Clara hadn't foreseen. That might make the decision of whether or not to relocate even more difficult. She'd been thinking about branching out and starting her own business, a much smaller business, and one that didn't have a whole lot of potential for growth, but painting was something she was passionate about and loved. If she was in love with her boss, and her boss returned her feelings, leaving his employment might be a little bit more difficult.

Although, Lana supposed that there was the off chance that he was catering to Clara just to get her to accept his offer.

Clara had never described him as the kind of man who would do something like that. Usually Clara wasn't a terrible judge of character, although Lana knew that her daughter had a tendency to be too trusting.

She liked to think that all the world was hearts and rainbows, and it just didn't work like that. But Lana could never find it in herself to dash any of Clara's hopes or dreams, because the world needed people like Clara. People who believed in the good and looked for it everywhere.

It seemed natural, but maybe Clara worked harder at focusing on the positive than Lana gave her credit for.

That night, Lana dreamed about Clara's wedding. It was on the beach at sunrise with long shadows and the crashing waves rolling in the mist.

Lana woke with a smile and a good feeling, although she couldn't help but be concerned for her child. She didn't suppose a mother ever stopped being concerned for her child.

Knowing that Jubilee would have everything under control, Lana slipped out for an early morning walk.

As she was walking down toward the beach, she was surprised to hear Clara calling her name.

"Mom! Wait!" Clara jogged up, sporting a sweatshirt but wearing shorts and flip-flops.

"You're up early," Lana said, smiling at her daughter and hooking her arm in hers.

"Every time I come here, I can't help but wake up with the sun or before it." She laughed, looking around at the sky that was barely light. "I love mornings on the beach."

"I do too. And now that Jubilee is helping with the bed-and-breakfast, I can take a walk, which is good for my physical health, but it also gives me a mental boost as well."

"I don't know anyone who needs a mental boost less than you do. You are the most positive and upbeat person I know."

"Have you ever met me?" Lana said, bumping Clara with her shoulder as they hit the beach and started walking north.

"Maybe you can introduce me later," Clara said, and they laughed and walked in silence for a bit.

Lana wasn't sure whether or not they would meet the older gentleman that she typically saw out along the beach area, and she supposed it didn't matter. It wasn't like Clara didn't know she walked on the beach, and the gentleman must be eighty if he was a year.

"So I finally met your boss. After all these years of hearing about him. He's younger than I thought he would be."

"He's older than me. He must be thirty-five at least."

"That's not too terribly much older than you. I bet you've overestimated that by a year or two. He's probably about the same age as Luke," Lana said, referring to her second son.

"Maybe. I guess… Actually, I know. I know when his birthday is. It's September seventeenth," and Clara rattled off the year, too, without even hesitating, as though it was a date that was seared into her memory.

Lana's arm tightened for a moment around Clara as she thought about the implications.

Clara obviously was his administrative assistant, and maybe she had to field calls from people giving him well wishes on his birthday, but for her to know the year and his exact age…

"I thought maybe you like him a little more in a personal way," Lana said cautiously. She didn't typically butt into her children's love lives, other than to remind them that she wasn't getting any younger and she wanted grandchildren while she was still young enough to enjoy them.

"I suppose I do. But we've always kept our relationship strictly professional. I've never even talked about anything personal with him, until yesterday."

"Makes sense. Although, I guess I didn't think to wonder until just now why he showed up in Strawberry Sands. Was it really just to look for property?"

"I don't know. He… He came to my tent, he bought all my paintings, Mom!" Clara pulled on her arm, and they stopped, facing each other. "He gave me fifty thousand dollars for the paintings that were left in my tent. That was after I had already sold at least thirty of them. Fifty thousand dollars!"

"Because he didn't want anyone else to buy them?" Lana said carefully, unsure what exactly that meant.

"No… I don't know." Clara emphasized her words with a headshake, and then she slipped her arm back through Lana's and they started walking on the beach again. "I really don't know."

"So…" Lana wasn't sure whether she should say anything about the look that she saw in Alex's eyes or not. She would be willing to bet quite a lot of money that Alex felt more for Clara than just strictly a professional feeling. Whether that feeling was tender friendship, or whether that feeling was…an attraction that would signal that he wanted a deeper and, hopefully, more meaningful relationship, she wasn't sure.

What she did know was, "He doesn't seem like the kind of man who will ever get married."

"Hmm. That could be true. I was just thinking yesterday that I've arranged more than a few dates for him, and it's never the same woman twice in a row. He has gone to dinners or shows or previews or premieres with the same woman once or twice, but never twice in a row."

"Interesting. So he has a thing against relationships."

Clara seemed like she might want to say more, and then she clamped her mouth closed.

"You don't have to tell me anything you're not comfortable sharing."

Clara sighed. "Yeah. I guess... I guess I just don't know. And this is muddying the waters even more for me, because he wanted me to go to the Cities but changed his mind yesterday, and now he's looking for property along the beach to buy so I can work here. Actually, so he and I can work from here. He's...going to work in Strawberry Sands just so I don't have to move to the Cities. What that means, I can't figure it out. And it makes it even harder because I was thinking about quitting, and somehow, he knew."

"He knew?" Lana said, surprised.

"Yes. He said he overheard something to that effect at the water cooler. And I have no reason to doubt that, but I just don't know what to do."

"I guess all you can do is pray about it and try to make the right decision."

"I spent a lot of time on my knees last night. I typically talk to the Lord a good bit, but I really had a lot of extra things to say to Him last night."

"Just be careful. He... He seems like the kind of man who would be possessive. Not in a bad way. I really don't think he's a bad man, but sometimes men who are powerful have trouble letting go of things that they think are theirs. He... He just might have trouble with the idea of letting go of you."

Lana didn't mean that as a warning exactly, she just wanted Clara to go into this with her eyes open, because she wanted to protect her daughter from getting hurt.

The lighthouse came into view, which was where Lana usually turned around, but not before she greeted the older gentleman who lived there.

Sure enough, at this time of morning, he was on the shore already, his fishing pole stuck in the sand, sitting in a beach chair beside it.

"Usually, I talk to this fellow before I turn around and walk back. That's all I have time for. But don't cut your walk short just because I have to get back."

"I thought I could help you in the kitchen a little bit this morning, Mom. Then, Mr.—uh, Alex," Clara cleared her throat like calling him Alex was uncomfortable, "is going to pick me up."

"For church?" Lana asked, unable to keep the surprise out of her voice.

"Yes. I got the feeling that he didn't normally go but that he wasn't completely unfamiliar with the idea. Maybe I can find out more."

"I suppose if you're going to move forward with any kind of relationship, that's an important thing to find out."

"I know. That was something I was praying about last night. I don't want to get emotionally involved with anyone, whether they're interested in me or not, if they aren't a Christian. Not because I'm a snob, but because... Well, the Bible says not to be unequally yoked with an unbeliever. So it's important he's a believer to begin with, but I guess I could see us arguing over those things in the future if we ever had children."

"You're a smart girl," Lana said, patting her daughter's arm and not bothering to disguise the pride in her voice.

Emotions were sometimes things which were very difficult to fight, and to have the foresight to know that a person had to go into a relationship with their eyes on the most important things was sometimes very difficult. Especially when a girl was Clara's age and unmarried. Potential boyfriends were fewer and further between than ever.

"Good morning, Mr. Pianse," Lana said as they got closer. "How are the fish biting this morning?"

"Terrible. I'll probably starve before nightfall." That was Mr. Pianse's standard answer to her, even if he had a whole string full of fish on the line he had staked in the lake.

"That's terrible. You be sure to come down to the bed-and-breakfast if you need something. I don't want you expiring from hunger just minutes away from a buffet feast that I would happily share with you."

"I might do that," he said, again, his standard answer, although he never took her up on it.

"Shouldn't you bring him some food?" Clara said as they turned around and started walking back down the beach.

"He doesn't like people to know this, but he probably has a whole string of fish on the stake he's got out in the lake." Lana nodded her head at the small orange flight that marked the spot.

"You're kidding."

"No. It's only our standard conversation that I insist he come eat at my place. I doubt he ever will. He catches plenty of fish anyway."

"Oh, I see."

"But he likes to pretend he doesn't have anything. I'm not sure whether that's because he doesn't want anyone to take his fishing spot, or whether that's just the way he talks all the time. Regardless, I come up here just to check on him, you know?"

"I see. So you never walk south, you always walk north?"

"Exactly. Neighbors have to watch out for each other after all," Lana said with a smile, knowing that Mr. Pianse might seem a little crusty and difficult, but she knew without a shadow of a doubt that if he ever heard that she needed anything, at the very least, he'd bring her some fish.

Chapter 9

"Obviously you can see that the owner spared no expense in the kitchen. Note the double oven, the stainless steel appliances, which all convey a modern style, and the tile floor." The real estate agent's voice droned on and on. Alex listened with half an ear. He didn't typically go into investments without checking everything out, and he wanted to be sure he didn't miss anything while looking at this home. But he was watching Clara.

She looked around and seemed interested, for sure, but she didn't look like she loved it.

Not like she looked when she looked at Lake Michigan. When she talked about her friends and family, when she showed him her mom's house and pointed at the tiny studio where she stayed.

He was looking for a hint on her face of any emotion, but it was almost as though she found the house cool and impersonal.

The tour continued as they followed the real estate agent up the stairs to the massive master bedroom with an equally massive attached bath and a closet that was as big as the room he had slept in last night. Bigger probably.

"Now, this is a little insider information that I'm probably not supposed to know," the real estate agent said, as though he were sharing some great secret. "There's a lawyer from Chicago who's thinking about purchasing this house. He's already seen it twice, and I suspect the only thing that's keeping him back is he has to juggle a few things so that he can spend the money without his wife knowing." The man looked smug as he lifted his brows, looking for their reactions to the gossip he just relayed, then he turned around and walked down the hall.

Clara did not seem impressed, and that honestly impressed Alex. She wasn't the kind of person to gossip on the job, and he liked that she didn't go for too much small-town gossip either.

He supposed she engaged in the typical back-and-forth that often happened in small towns where people talked about other people's business, but Clara had always stayed away from speculation and insinuation.

They checked out the basement, and then they enjoyed the lake view from the porch before they got in their separate cars and drove to the schoolhouse. It was just a five-minute drive away, a little out of sight of the mansion that they just toured.

"What did you think?" he asked as they were on their way with the real estate agent leading in his car.

"It was big."

"That's it? It was big?"

"Well, there is plenty of room for an office. And you have a nice view."

"It would be your view too. This would be the office that we would share." He wasn't sure why it was so important to him that she understood that.

"Of course. And it wouldn't be far from my home."

"Would you find some place to buy? If you were going to live here full-time?" The attic room or her tiny cottage wasn't much if she were going to stay in it all the time.

"I don't know. I don't really need much. And if I were here all the time, I'd be helping Mom with the bed-and-breakfast, so I wouldn't need a kitchen."

"That's where you packed our lunch this morning?"

She'd packed a lunch for them, and they'd eaten after church. Church wasn't as bad as what he was afraid it was going to be. The message was actually pretty good and made him realize that maybe he had drifted away from the Lord, or maybe he'd never been as close to God as what he should have been.

It inspired him to want to make some changes, but he tucked all those ideas away to examine later. He didn't want to do anything rash. Being a Christian had a tendency to change people's lives, and he didn't want to be one of those people. The kind of person who was unrecognizable after having a relationship or whatever it was with God. He just wanted to do enough to skate himself into heaven and maybe do a little good while he was on earth.

"Yeah. I mean, of course I would talk to Mom about it first, but she's always okay with it. Especially because I help her every chance I get."

"I see." He didn't understand the whole family dynamic. It was still a bit of a mystery to him. Even at church, Clara had been hugging and laughing and talking to pretty much everyone, and it was a friendly, noncompetitive type of group that made him feel...like an outsider looking in. Except, people just accepted that he was with Clara. They seemed to understand that they weren't together together, but that he was her...friend or something.

It had been kind of nagging at the back of his head that he wanted to put more of a label on what was between them, but he also understood that because of their working relationship, pushing for that could be dangerous. He could end up completely losing her. And he certainly didn't want that.

Honestly, for the first time in his life, he wasn't sure what he wanted.

He pulled in beside the realtor who was already parked in the school parking lot.

"That used to be the playground over there." She nodded at a weedy spot over behind the building. The building wasn't excessively small, but it was much smaller than the mansion they'd just visited. And a lot more run down.

"Looks like everything's been carted away or has fallen down."

"Yeah," Clara said, and she sounded sad. Maybe she'd want to bring everything back and build it up to its former glory. He wasn't sure what it was about her, but whatever she wanted, he wanted to do it for her.

"All right, I don't know much about this property except it's being sold as is," the realtor said, obviously not wanting to sell this property to them. It was one million dollars cheaper than the one they had just seen, for starters, and his commission would be much less.

But as they were walking toward the front steps, that light Alex had been looking for on Clara's face, the one that had been missing when they looked at the mansion, now shone brightly in her eyes.

"I've walked up these steps so many times. I sat on them talking to my friends. I always loved sitting here looking at the lake."

Sure enough, the front of the building faced the lake, and the view was glorious.

"I was told that the doors probably weren't locked."

"I can't imagine they are. Or they would have trouble with vandalism."

"We don't usually have too much trouble with vandalism in Strawberry Sands. It's just not that big."

"Oh?" the realtor said with interest, looking at Clara. "You're from around here?"

There were no realty agencies in Strawberry Sands, so most likely the realtor was from Blueberry Beach or somewhere further away. He hadn't checked when he booked the appointment.

"I am. I've lived here my whole life. I went to this school."

"That's what you were saying. So that's why you're interested in it?" His brows drew down, and he looked between the two of them again, as though wondering if there was something more between them.

It made Alex want to put his arm around Clara or do something else to let the realtor know that she was not available.

That wasn't right. Because he didn't have any right to do that, any claim to stake, other than as her employer, and even that was skating on thin ice.

"Well then, maybe you should be the one to offer the tour."

"I don't know. It's been such a long time," Clara said as they stepped into the building. "But it still smells the same." She breathed deeply and closed her eyes as though imagining herself back as a young child, running through the doors with her friends, smiling and laughing.

"There's an office on the left and an office on the right. And then, you go the whole way back, and you can either turn left or right to get into either classroom. If you go straight back and through the doors, that's the gymnasium. It's small. Smaller than a basketball court, but that's where we had our assemblies, and it's where we played in the winter."

"Interesting. I've never seen a school this small."

"I guess it was more cost-effective for the state of Michigan to close all the small schools and bus the kids to a central location. I guess less overhead for staff or something. But I think we miss something whenever we take kids out of their hometown and just dump them all together. I know going to high school wasn't nearly the great experience that going to elementary school was. In fact, my grades went down, and I stopped loving school."

"I see. You went from being a big fish in a little pond to a little fish in a big pond."

"Maybe. But it really wasn't the loss of notoriety, it was more... You lost that friendly everybody knows everybody else kind of feeling. It was... We didn't have turf wars or anything, but we all came from different areas, and we wanted to cling to the people that were comfortable and familiar. I suppose that's human nature, and that's good in a way. After all, humans do better whenever we have a family and a community behind us. The idea of diversity making us stronger is not necessarily a true statement."

He had never heard anyone talk like that, and he wanted to call her on it. Wanted to tell her that was almost heresy, but it really wasn't. As he thought about it more, she was right.

Humans had a tendency to split themselves into groups. Whether it was gangs in Chicago, or companies, or football teams, or whatever it was that people liked or rooted for, they felt a kinship with other folks around them who were rooting for the same thing. It was what humans did. Why not do it with the community and family? He had been preached at for so long that diversity was better, and the idea of having a deep sense of family and community was almost a foreign notion, this thing that Clara said so easily.

"This was the side for the young kids." Clara opened the door, and they looked around.

It would make a great office. In fact, they could split it into several offices. Or they could use the two offices out front, and the bigger rooms could be...bedrooms or kitchens or... If he did enough work, he could turn this into a house. He had wanted to have an office in his home where he could stay and work.

He kept that idea tucked in the back of his head as they finished looking at the school. Since the door wasn't locked, they thanked the realtor for his time and told him they'd be in touch.

Clara seemed loath to leave, and he couldn't blame her. She'd been enjoying the trip down memory lane, remembering the things that she'd done as a child, her friends and fun times she had.

But as they stood, looking out the front windows at the beautiful view of the lake, he said, "I have a question for you."

"Okay," she said, looking at him with a bemused smile on her face.

"Should I buy this and turn it into offices and a home? Or should I buy this and turn it into all offices and buy the house we looked at first to live in?"

Chapter 10

"You know what? Never mind. I know what I'm going to do."

Alex said that before Clara was able to answer his question about which house he should buy.

The nicer home they looked at first was the obvious choice. The schoolhouse was going to take a lot of renovation. He could use the offices almost right away, but the building was old, it needed a new roof, they didn't know what shape the septic was in, and if he was going to live in it, there were a lot of things that were going to need to be added and fixed.

The other house was move-in ready.

Clara had been raised to be practical, even if she was more of a dreamer than a practical woman. Still, she could be practical when she needed to.

She nodded, looking once more out the front windows at the view of the lake. She could imagine sitting there, with her easel and paints, looking up at the lake for inspiration as she put the picture in her mind on the canvas.

"I have to go to the Cities tomorrow." Apparently, Alex was ready for a subject change. "I'll discuss details with the real estate agent, and I'll have him put an offer in first thing tomorrow morning. We'll get things rolling here, and you can go to Chicago and start packing. I want my office packed up, yours, and anything you know we need in the meeting and storage rooms."

"Yes, sir," Clara said. A bit of relief washed over her as he settled back into the role of boss and she assumed her normal role of business subordinate. A subordinate who might be a little bit in love with her boss, but that felt familiar too. It was a little, secret thing that she kept tucked away. It wasn't something that was out in the open or that she was afraid was going to come out in the open the way she'd been the last couple of days.

Hopefully they would move here, and everything would continue just the way it had been. There was a reason why things were called a "comfort zone." Moving out of it was most definitely uncomfortable, and she honestly wasn't sure she wanted to. It was one thing to admire him from afar, it was another thing to have all of the feelings and emotions and uncertainties of not knowing where she stood with him and wondering if their relationship was going to move forward, only to explode.

"Clara?"

"Yes?" She turned and saw him staring at her. She got the feeling that he had been staring for some time.

"I want you to stay with me."

Oh. She totally forgot about that. She was considering starting her own business. Everything felt so comfortable and safe when she was with him, taking orders from him, doing what he wanted, and just thinking about her dreams, but not acting on them.

"Promise me?" His words did not have his normal confidence, almost as though he knew he was asking for more than what he should. Wanting her to give him more than an employee typically needed to. She'd given him seven years of loyalty. She didn't owe him anything more.

"You're moving here because of me. Spending a lot of money, and uprooting everything you have, changing your plans, and doing something that you totally weren't expecting." She stopped. Why was he doing all of this for her? Just because he didn't want to train another secretary? "How much time, beyond the seven years I've already given you, is right for me to give, in order to justify the way you're changing everything for me?"

"That's a good question. I guess you really don't owe me anything. Seven years was more than enough."

She wasn't sure exactly what they were saying, but it felt like there was a message going between them that hadn't been there before. Like he was acknowledging that things were shifting. Or maybe she was. Or maybe he figured out that she felt more for him than what a secretary should. But that didn't explain why he was switching things up just for her.

She gathered all the courage that she contained, and she said, "Why? Why are you doing this?"

She felt like she was good at her job. She tried hard to be good at her job in fact. But he wasn't going to recoup the losses that he was going to take by making the changes he was going to be doing.

His jaw flexed as his eyes met hers steadily, then something shifted there before his whole body turned toward the lake. He seemed to search the horizon for the answers to the question that she hadn't even meant to ask.

"I know I told you that you could ask me anything, and I would tell you. But I guess I can't really tell you the answer if I don't know it myself."

He turned back to look at her, and while there was no insecurity on his face, it wasn't the usual confidence that she was used to. There was a softness there, in the crinkle of his eyes and turn of his lips, that she wasn't used to seeing.

"I guess if I figure out why, I'll let you know." There was a short pause, then he lifted his chin just a fraction. "And I don't need any promises from you. I've already decided what I'm going to do, and I'm going to do it regardless of what you do. Are you good for tomorrow?"

She nodded slowly, although it took her a couple of moments to figure out exactly what she was supposed to do tomorrow.

That's right. Go to Chicago, pack up the offices. It would take up most of the week.

"Once I talk to the realtor, we'll figure out when we can close. Probably Friday. It won't take long since I'm paying cash, and I have a great lawyer. Once I know for sure, I'll send you the information so you can order the moving trucks."

She nodded. "All right."

"I'll be in the Cities, but you know you can always get a hold of me if you need me."

Normally it was him getting a hold of her, so she didn't quite know what to say. Turned out she didn't need to say anything, because he spoke again.

"Thanks for sharing a little of your history with me. It's been interesting getting to know you this weekend. I... I enjoyed it."

Her mouth dropped open, and she didn't have the presence of mind to close it.

"Come on. I'll drive you back to your mom's. I need to head to the airport."

"All right."

She felt unbalanced, unsteady. Like she was walking over ground she had never tried before. Which was exactly what was going on.

They didn't say much on the ride back to her mom's house, and he left shortly after.

She couldn't shake the feeling that something had changed in their relationship, but she didn't know what to do about it. Didn't know if that was the direction she wanted to go. And it was so difficult to read him. But knowing the bit of his past that she'd found out this weekend had changed the way she saw him completely.

After she stripped the bed in the attic room and started that load of laundry, she went back to her small cottage and got ready to leave in the morning.

Chapter 11

The week was a physical one, with Clara packing up boxes of books and papers and all the things that made up an office for both Alex and for her. In the seven years that she'd known him, the office in the high-rise in downtown Chicago overlooking Lake Michigan had been his home base. She could hardly believe that he was taking everything and moving it.

Her office was a little easier to pack up, and it was a little easier for her to believe that she was moving. So, Wednesday evening at nine o'clock, she had her office completely finished and had about ten boxes full of things that she had packed from his office. She was sitting in front of the bookshelf, a box beside her, carefully taking volumes off and putting them in the box when the door opened and her head jerked around. Her heart leapt to her throat, because she thought she was alone.

"You're still working," Alex said as he walked in carrying a bag from a Chinese take-out place just down the street.

"Yeah. I was...hoping to get everything done by Thursday evening so I could go home Friday."

She'd often worked extra during the week, and oftentimes when she'd done that, he'd given her Friday or Monday off so she could have a long weekend at home. It was normal and not something she even really discussed with him anymore. As long as she put in as much time as he needed her to, he was fine with her taking time off when things got slow.

"Is your office finished?" He came over, the bag crinkling as he set it down on his desk. It still looked the same as it had when he left, since she hadn't touched it.

"Yeah. I started mine first. It was a little bit easier for me to...believe that I was leaving. But packing up your office...feels weird. This is where you belong."

Not just in his office. But in Chicago. In the city. A man like him, someone who was used to commanding things and wielding his power and being a mover and shaker didn't belong in a tiny little place like Strawberry Sands.

She thought that maybe he knew what she was saying, because as she set another book in the box, he came over and stood in front of the floor-to-ceiling window that overlooked the lake. Night had fallen, but the lights of the city reflected from the clouds, and they could see the waves rolling in and hitting the shore walk, the whitecaps reflecting the neon lights, and a few people braving the wind and darkness.

"The view's a little different on the other side of the lake," he said, and it almost sounded like he was having a casual conversation with her. Normally they talked business. Except for last weekend.

"Yeah. A little wilder. A little more desolate."

"Desolate. I don't think that's the way I would describe Strawberry Sands. There is a...community. A feeling of fellowship or something."

She remembered the way he was raised. With parents who were in and out of jail, drug users, parents who allowed their only child to drink alcohol for the entertainment of their friends. Her fingers curled. She could hardly stand thinking about that. Someone should take them and throw them in jail, except...that's where she was. What would it be like to have a mother who was in jail?

She knew what it was like to have a father who was absent, although somewhere in the world, her dad still walked the earth. His didn't. That was a total shift and an important one.

She set the book in, pulling her hand from the box and looking out at the view he stared at.

"Strawberry Sands is a special place." She believed that, but of course that was what someone who had grown up there would think.

"It is. I... I appreciate you introducing me to it. I..." His voice trailed off, and he didn't say anything else.

She didn't know what to say or do. This was all new to her. She'd spent the last three days trying to figure out what was going on in their relationship.

He hadn't called her, hadn't texted other than the typical business texts he normally sent—of ordering her to check paper supplies and to check into things like garbage pickup and office cleaning in Strawberry Sands, and she'd called about internet for that area as well.

"I don't think I told you, but I talked to the realtor and submitted an offer on Sunday evening. It was accepted right away. I actually offered half of what they were asking, and I suppose it should give me pause that they didn't even blink an eye. But they didn't. And I didn't, either. Just wanting to move ahead as fast as I could. We're closing Friday."

Clara gasped. "Friday? The day after tomorrow?"

He grinned a little. A satisfied grin, one she'd seen a few times over the years when he'd done especially well with a business deal. Then he spoke as he moved to the desk and started pulling things out of the take-out bag.

"We're paying cash, so we don't have to go through all the things the bank would require. I've got other things I've set in motion, too. We're getting permits, lining up contractors, and I'm going to be doing some work on my own. I have a storage trailer that's going to be sitting on the property, and we're going to be moving all the stuff from the offices there. So we can get it all moved in when we're able."

"Wait. What? What property did you buy?"

He paused with a small white napkin in his hand. "The schoolhouse."

Her mouth dropped again. She had assumed he was buying the house. The schoolhouse was a foolish decision. There was so much work to do. He couldn't move in right away... There was so much to do, who knew when they would be able to move in.

"You bought the schoolhouse?"

"Yes. That was the one you wanted."

Since when did he do what she wanted? What was going on? It wasn't like he was doing any kind of underhanded business that he needed her to keep secret so he was trying to appease her. She knew no business secrets that she could spread to the world that would get him in trouble or even undermine him in any way.

"You know, if I leave, I'm not going to talk about anything that's happening here."

"Of course not. You signed an NDA when you started."

"Even if I hadn't. I wouldn't blab."

"I know." He grabbed a fork and carried it along with two cartons over to her, handing a carton and a fork to her. "Shrimp lo mein."

It was her favorite. She couldn't believe it. In all the years that they'd eaten takeout together, and there had been more than a few times where they worked late at the office and ordered in, he had never been the one doing the ordering. It had always been her.

"I can't believe you know."

"April seventeenth." He rattled off the year as well.

"You looked that up."

"No. I knew it. I just didn't want you to know that I knew, because..."

"Why? Because what?" she prompted when he trailed off.

"Because I can't tell you anyone else's birthday." His eyes met hers, but not with confidence, almost as though he was forcing himself to lift them from the floor or they were so heavy they just wanted to sink into the ground.

Her breath caught in her throat again. The feeling was starting to become familiar. He kept surprising her.

"You did?" She trusted him. She'd seen him do business. She'd seen him refuse to lie even when it would be more convenient, even at times where it really wouldn't be considered a huge lie, just a little nudge of the truth, and he refused.

"Yeah." His lips pulled back, and he didn't look super happy about it.

But he didn't say anything more, just walked back to the desk, grabbed the two bottles of water, and came back and sat down beside her, the box between them.

"This feels a little familiar. Only the last time, we were looking at the lake from the other side."

"And there were ants and bugs, and I had you sitting on the ground without even a blanket."

"I didn't mind. It was the first time I'd ever had an outdoor picnic, and I have to say, I might have gotten addicted to the occurrence."

"You never had a picnic outside before?"

"This is the second time in my adult life that I've eaten on the ground. I did it a good bit when I was a kid. But never outside."

She closed her mouth. Somehow it was so hard to imagine the man in front of her as a little kid being shuffled around by his parents. And used. He might not want to admit it, but he had been abused. Maybe they hadn't hit him, but allowing a small child to get drunk was most definitely child abuse, in her book anyway.

"It's a wonder you didn't grow up to be an alcoholic."

"I don't drink. Or I probably would be." He opened the container and stared at his food for a moment. "I suppose we should pray for this."

The pastor had said something in his sermon about thanking God for everything, including their food. She knew Alex had been listening. He always listened. He might not agree, he might be thinking of arguments in his head or might even be creating a whole world where nothing went along with whatever the speaker was saying, but he always listened. He said more than once that you don't know what you don't know, and you don't know what you might learn from someone else.

"I suppose we should. You want me to?" she asked, figuring that what he had said was a hint for her.

"I can."

Instead of allowing her eyes to widen, she dropped her chin and closed them. He was going to pray for their food? That was new. In all the times they'd eaten together, she wasn't even sure he'd ever waited for her to get her food out before taking a forkful and continuing to work while he ate on the side.

A few long seconds ticked by before his voice broke the silence. "Lord God, thank you. For the food. For the company. Most especially for the company. And for the new direction You've given me. Amen."

His words were short, but they didn't hold any insecurity, and he didn't look to her to see what her reaction would be, as though he wasn't sure how his words would be received. It was like he was only saying them for the Lord, and she just happened to be sitting there with him and happened to hear them. She felt like she'd seen a little glimpse of his heart.

He felt like God had given him a new direction?

Chapter 12

Clara felt like it might be prying to question him about his prayer if she asked him about what he'd just prayed. After all, it was a conversation between the Lord and him. Although, he'd allowed her to listen in.

"You know, I hadn't gone to church in years before I went on Sunday."

That didn't surprise her, and as she opened her box of food, she just nodded.

"But the pastor said so many things that resonated with me. That were what I believe, unconsciously or not."

"That align with your worldview?" she asked.

He nodded. "And I didn't realize how much of that worldview was formed when I was exposed to church when I was a kid."

"You rode the bus to church?"

"My parents certainly didn't take me, but in inner-city Chicago, there are lots of churches that pick kids up and take them to Sunday school. I got involved in one of those and went off and on through junior high. After that, it wasn't cool. I really loved the teachings, though. It all made sense to me. And while everything else that you learn in the world is pretty much the opposite of what you learn from the Bible, somehow those teachings stuck with me. I... I admit that I spent a lot of time in the Cities doing some research."

"Research into the Bible?" she asked as she stuck her fork into her lo mein and twirled it around.

"Yeah. Into why I might believe that it was true. After all, it seems like if I believe that there is a God, it makes sense that He left directions for us. Those directions would be the Bible. And if I believe those two things, then it would make sense that I should follow the Bible. Right?"

"Well, yeah. When you put it like that. I think a lot of people don't have any idea of what the Bible says. Christians don't even know."

"It's a little intimidating to start reading. Someone ought to break it up into sixty-six separate books so that you don't feel like you're running a marathon while you're trying to read."

"I don't know that anyone's ever thought of that, but if you read the Gospels, you get the gist of what Jesus taught."

"We don't see the whole picture. See, I'm a global thinker. I like to see everything, the whole picture, and then I break it down into components so that I can build based on what I see in my head as the end result. I need to see the big picture before I break it down into the smaller action items."

"Action items meaning..."

"The way God wants us to live. Basically, a day by day, hour by hour, thought by thought way of living."

"Aren't you missing something?"

"Salvation?"

She nodded. Following the Bible was mostly meaningless unless a person had completely bought into Christianity. In order to do that, they had to acknowledge Jesus as God's Son and accept his free gift of salvation. It was an easy concept, simple to understand, but hard for so many because it required repentance which was turning from their way of life, following after sin and self, and turning toward the Savior, committing their life to him.

That was the holdup for so many.

Believing wasn't hard. Accepting a gift wasn't hard, either. That turning, that conversion, that repentance, the humbleness that required, the admittance of shame and guilt and the knowledge that a person couldn't save himself, then giving oneself to God for His use... That was where people stumbled.

"A lot of times, pride gets in the way. I've often watched as people who are full of pride walk away from the Lord because they just can't bend their knee."

"I don't know that I could have done it when I was younger. I think... I look back, sometimes God takes us on the path and then brings things into our lives at just the right time. If this would have happened...even a year ago, I might not have been ready. But now? I guess I've learned enough to know that I don't know nearly as much as I thought I knew when I started, and I will never know it all."

She chewed on her lo mein, looking into the dark night, seeing the rolling waves and the lights of the city to the left. It seemed a little surreal that she was sitting in the office on the floor with her boss and he was talking about...getting saved. Repentance. Becoming a Christian. Living a life of service to God. They never talked about religion, and although she knew his politics, they didn't talk about that, either.

"Are you going to tell me that you just believe? You never question anything?"

She lifted her shoulder, not sure what to say. "I watched my mom live what she believed. What she taught us to believe. She made God seem so real that I never thought to question that He wasn't. I can see Him in my room. I guess I just look at the lake and I can see God in it. Look at the storms rolling in, and I can't imagine all that just happening. To believe that it just happened out of nothing takes so much more faith than it does to believe that there is a God who controls it all.

"And I suppose the thing that my mom did that really helped me, and where some of my friends went wrong, was that a lot of my friends thought that being a Christian meant you were happy all the time, bad things didn't happen to you, and if God loved you, then you weren't going to suffer. My mom made sure that I understood that being a Christian meant bad things probably were going to happen to you, that you were going to suffer, and that God allowed you to in order for you to grow and become more like Him. She emphasized that the hard times were the times where you became more like Jesus or you chose to try to do things without Him."

"I see." He took a breath and used his fork to poke around in his box without actually picking anything up and eating it. "In a way, I agree with you, but I can also sit here in my mind and think, did God really want a little boy to go through the things I went through? And of course, there was no one teaching me that those were things that were going to shape me, but as you say that, I realize that they did. Those things did make me stronger. They did form the determination that I had in my heart to become who I am today. Although, I lost God along the way for a while."

"I think we all do. I mean, not everyone, but we're human. We want to do things our own way. We get to a point in our lives where we think we can do it without God, or maybe we don't even make a conscious decision, we just start doing things we want rather than thinking about what God wants. I have. I know a lot of times in my life, I just looked at the choices in front of me and picked the best thing that I thought was going to make me the happiest, or make me the most money, or maybe the most comfortable. I didn't think about choosing to do the things that God wants me to do. And maybe even more importantly, choosing to not do the things that I know God doesn't want me to do."

"For some of us, that means giving up a lot of things."

"Yeah. Some people think that God is just kind of in the sky and uninterested in us, but He wants every second to be accounted for. Not that we can't have our rest or relaxation, but we have a tendency to place a priority on resting and relaxing when we're here on earth to work. Our relaxing time is in heaven."

"Every seventh day, God commanded us to rest."

"I think it was God's way of letting us know that we can't work all the time. And I do think that God wants us to enjoy ourselves. However we do that. But so many times, enjoying ourselves means sinning."

"Yeah." Neither one of them said anything. They really didn't have to. They'd worked in an office setting for years and knew that after-work drinks often led to after-work other things, things that broke up marriages and destroyed relationships, and even if they didn't do that, things that were not right.

It was commonplace. Every day. These wicked things that people didn't even blink at anymore, and in fact, it was the people who didn't do the wicked things that were looked at as an aberration.

"When I was in the Cities, instead of starting what I was planning on starting, I took the first steps toward closing it all down."

His words were a shock to her.

"You keep saying things that surprise me. I... Pretty much every time you open your mouth, I can't believe what you're saying."

He laughed. "What are you talking about?"

"You...changed. You're just...not the same."

"Isn't that what was supposed to happen?"

Now he was talking about religion again. Conversion. Being different.

"I hadn't considered. I... I always thought it was a, you know, you're gonna look like a monk or something. But you're right. Since Sunday morning, you've been different, and I never thought that was why."

"Jesus changes people. Maybe sometimes he changes them quickly, and sometimes some of us are a little bit slower, but we change."

"Yeah. Which makes me wonder if I've changed."

"If you were saved when you were young, maybe it's not the same because you grow up trying to walk with Jesus, and the growth that you show as you get older will be growth toward Jesus. But there is a big change if you're older when you get saved."

"Good point," she said, knowing that what he said was true. If she had been a Christian since she was young, her whole life should have been building on that foundation. With no great changes necessary. Just small adjustments as she got off course.

"You are okay with the change?"

"You just keep saying things and surprising me. This is the first time since I started working for you that instead of expanding your business, you're...contracting."

"I don't need to do what I've been doing. I haven't been enjoying it for a while. I suppose the time in Strawberry Sands showed me that, and the time in church reminded me that there are other things that are more important. Things that I've been neglecting. People. People are important."

"Exactly."

"The problem is, I don't always enjoy being around people."

"Me, either."

"But there's a community in Strawberry Sands, a community of people who help each other. There is no law that says that you have to have millions of people you're helping. You can just be a blessing to the people around you, even if there's only fifty or a hundred of them in your community."

She never thought it through like that, but it was true. People didn't have to light up the whole world. They only had to light their corner of it.

Jesus didn't command them to be a light that shone for everyone, just for the people who saw them.

"The people who see you should see you as different, but you don't have to go around trying to make everyone in the world see you."

"That's so true."

They sat a little in silence, and then she said, "Do you need me to help schedule contractors? Or to start redoing the interior? I'm sure you want to get moved in as soon as you can."

"I've actually been arranging things while I was in the Cities." He stared at the piece of chicken on his fork. "I've been moving things around so I can take some time off."

"Take some time...off?" She repeated what he said, even though she heard him, just because she found it so unbelievable. In the seven years that she'd known him, she hadn't known him to take any time off, at all, ever. One year, he even called her on Christmas. He hadn't realized what day it was.

"Yeah."

"So you're going to arrange all the contractors?"

"When I was about twelve, my uncle came in and tried to straighten out my home. My mom was in jail, my dad was pretty much a loser, but my uncle tried to get him sobered up and put him to work in his contracting business."

"Well, that's good," Clara said hesitantly, because he wasn't talking like it was going to be a good thing.

"It should have been. It should have been the best thing that ever happened to me. But it wasn't."

"How?" she interrupted him.

"Well, first, I spent the next five years working for my uncle. I even got special permission to get out of school early my junior and senior years. It was around Christmastime, I think, my senior year that my dad and uncle got into a fight. Dad wasn't a dependable worker, never had been, but as long as Uncle Bob was there, he'd had a semblance of a job. Those were probably the most stable years of my life. Mom got out of jail, then ended up getting caught for shoplifting with a weapon, and she went back. Anyway, Dad and Uncle Bob had an argument, and... Dad ended up shooting Uncle Bob." Alex's voice was rather dispassionate. There wasn't much emotion in it at all, although his words made Clara gasp.

"Uncle Bob didn't die right away, but they arrested Dad immediately. Anyway, I visited Uncle Bob a couple times in the hospital. He ended up showing me the backend of his business, paperwork and all that stuff, which of course I hated. What kid likes that? But while he was in the hospital, and he knew he was most likely going to die, he told me that I had a good head on my shoulders."

Chapter 13

One side of his mouth turned up into a lopsided grin. "It was the first time anyone had told me anything like that. Maybe it went to my head. Anyway, he said I should go to college for business."

"You're brilliant. How could people not tell you that you were brilliant?"

"My grades in school reflected my homework. No one cared whether I did well or not, including myself. I just wanted to play, like most kids. But I didn't want to end up like my dad, and Uncle Bob pointed out to me that if I wasn't going to end up like him, I had to make some changes. I couldn't live his life, I had to forge my own path. And he told me that there wasn't going to be anyone there to guide me. I was going to have to do it myself."

"That's harsh."

"He was dying. Dad was going to be in prison. It was true."

"That's sad."

Alex shrugged his shoulder like it didn't really matter. "It's one of those hard things, remember? The thing that is going to make me stronger? I mean, I guess it didn't have to, but I determined that I would do what Uncle Bob suggested. I... I didn't want to be my dad. I didn't want to shoot someone, especially someone I really loved, and then spend the rest of my life in prison. And my dad was a pretty tough dude, but he was scared to death of going to prison."

Alex paused there. He pursed his lips and then said, "I guess for good reason. He died there."

That's right. She'd forgotten that he told her his dad died while in prison.

"All right. Enough with the unhappy thoughts. Anyway, the point was, it's been a long time since I've done construction work, but I know how to do it. I think... I think I'd like to get back to that. I... I ended up going in a different direction in college, which was maybe a good thing. And I don't regret that. But I'd forgotten that sometimes life can be simple and you can be happy. Or maybe I never knew it. I think I'd like to try that."

Clara blinked. "I can agree with that. Life can be simple, and you can be happy. I think, I always believed anyway, that you could choose to be happy, choose to be content. But honestly, with a life like that, I'm not sure."

"Weren't you listening? It's the hard times that make us stronger. Sure, a different life would be nice, but... I wouldn't be where and what I am today if I hadn't had those hard knocks."

She pressed her lips together. She wasn't sure whether she would want to be where he was if she had to go through what he had gone through. But once a person was through it, they could look back and learn. They didn't have to look back and live through it again. His attitude was best, and she could admit that, even as she knew she wasn't sure she would have survived his childhood.

"You know, there's a difference between you and me." His words were casual like he was just pointing out something that wasn't obvious, although she had to fight back a snort, because of course they were different. "You're soft. You flutter around, all happy, smiling at people, trusting people. You're really quick to lend a helping hand, and you're eager to do what you can to be a blessing to people. I'm a lot harder. More demanding. I take life with both hands, and I wrestle it into submission. Maybe that's a difference in our childhoods. But I think I'm tired of wrestling. I think I want to let go of life and maybe just float for a bit. Not float as in give up, but float as in...let God wrestle with my life while I just hold on to Him and let Him pull me wherever He wants to."

"Wow. That's... That's beautiful. That's exactly what I think we're supposed to do as Christians. We're not supposed to stress and worry and strive the way we do. Although, I really don't think there's anything wrong with working hard."

"Me either. And I intend to work hard getting the schoolhouse in shape. But there's a difference between working hard and stressing while you're doing it. Always with your eyes on something else, never content with what you have been given."

Clara couldn't disagree.

"I just want to thank you for helping me with that. Helping me see that. Taking me to Strawberry Sands and reminding me that there is more to life than what I was currently living for."

She wanted to ask if him losing his dad and his mom and his uncle and the complete lack of any kind of anchor in his childhood was the reason that he didn't seem to have any relationships, not just romantic relationships, but friendship relationships. He seemed to be very much alone. And she wondered if that was the reason. If it was a deliberate thing on his part, or if it was something that he had unconsciously done.

But she wasn't sure what words to use. And wasn't sure it was any of her business anyway.

"I scared you?" he said after they had been eating in silence for a while, and his fork scraped the bottom of his cardboard box.

"No. I guess you just gave me a lot to think about. I sometimes wonder what makes people tick, you know? And I thought that maybe your childhood has made it so that it's difficult for you to have solid relationships because you never really had them when you were a kid." She sighed. "Or never really had anyone who truly cared about you. Cared that good things happen to you. Like a parent should. A kid isn't for their parents' entertainment, although I think parents love to watch their children. But a child is supposed to be something the parent cares about and wants to see the best for them. And we grow up, knowing that is what we put into our relationships. Loving the people who are our friends and family and doing things so they know that we want the best for them."

"Maybe. I guess I never really thought about it. I... I don't feel comfortable in relationships and... Maybe that's why. Maybe I feel like they're not going to last." He swallowed and set his carton down on the floor. He stretched his legs out and put his hands behind him. "Maybe people just leave, and I just expect that."

She felt a little guilty, because she had been thinking about leaving. He had been the only thing that had kept her from quitting her job. That probably was information that wouldn't help him in any way, so she closed her lips around it.

"But maybe, maybe I just needed to have a relationship with Jesus and develop that before I worked on having relationships with people. Because most of the time, we have relationships based on what other people do for us. And we don't really think about what we can do for them. At least I don't. You're different."

"It's kind of my job to think about what I can do for you. So don't give me any credit."

"You help your mom without getting paid for it. You encouraged Griff in his endeavor to make the best stuff he can. You encouraged Chi in her business of owning the diner. I've watched you over the years help your siblings, your friends, and your coworkers. And I know it's your job to help me, but you always go above and beyond what I ask you to do. I've never said anything, because after a while I just expected it, but the idea of losing you, of hiring someone who is just your run-of-the-mill administrative assistant, made me realize how much of a blessing I truly had in you."

He seemed like he wanted to say more, but he closed his mouth and stared out the window.

She didn't really know what to say. She supposed when she watched him, she often got the impression that for him, it was all about making money, getting bigger, being more successful. Whatever that looked like at the time. Whether it was acquiring more or selling to the highest bidder.

"I'm flying back down to the Cities tomorrow."

"You flew in just for today?"

He stilled beside her, almost seemed to stop breathing, and then his head turned to her. "Yeah. I just wanted to come see you."

Her eyes widened, and her fork froze in midair. He had flown the whole way from Minneapolis to Chicago, which wasn't an excessive distance, but flying was a hassle, and he had done it just for her?

"Did you have something you needed to talk about?" she asked, knowing that they'd just spent the last hour talking, but not about anything that was so important he would have to fly home in order to do it.

He stared at her for a bit while his chest rose and fell. Her heart pounded so loud she thought surely he could hear it.

"Is it so amazing that I would come back, just to see you?"

"Well, yeah." It was. "Flying is a huge hassle and a pain in the butt, plus it takes a lot of time, and I know you're busy and—and..."

"Maybe I missed you."

Her mouth was open, and she froze with it that way. The words that she was going to say dying in her throat as she blinked.

Alexander Hudson, her boss, had just almost said that he missed her. Almost. He said maybe he did.

"Did you?" she asked softly.

"Clara. I followed you to Strawberry Sands. I went house hunting with you." He laughed a little and shook his head. "I stayed at your mom's house. I followed you around the small-town festival like a puppy dog on a leash." He closed his eyes and grunted again. "I don't know what's wrong with me, but yeah. I was sitting in the Cities, and all I could think about was that you were probably here, you were probably working late, and I hated that you weren't beside me where I could talk to you. Ask you what you thought. I missed that...security I have when you're beside me. I know, of all the people in the world, that you have my best interests at heart."

He looked over at her, and she knew she needed to get the stunned look off her face, but she couldn't.

But he hadn't said anything about holding any kind of affection for her. About liking her. It was all about him liking what she did for him.

He hadn't said anything about her as a person. Not really. She was...getting excited over nothing.

"You were the one person in the world I have a relationship with who I trust."

That couldn't be true. He had his business partners. He had the people that he worked with. But she supposed they were all under contract. Technically so was she. He had just mentioned the NDA that she had signed before she even started to work.

"I don't know what to say," she finally said.

"You don't have to say anything," he said, although he sounded disappointed. He'd wanted something from her, but she didn't know what it was. She didn't know how to give him what he wanted without risking a lot of pain on her end. He didn't understand that her emotions were involved in their relationship. He just thought it was a business arrangement, one where he could trust her, one where he didn't want to let her go. One where she was there for him. And he didn't know that she felt more.

"Are you done?" He nodded at her carton.

"Yeah." She wasn't the slightest bit hungry anymore. He reached over to take the carton from her, and she lifted it up to hand it to him. His hand gripped from one side, her fingers squeezed the other, but he didn't pull it away. Just held it between them while he looked in her eyes.

"I'm afraid I might be a little intense," he finally said.

"You can be quite intimidating. I don't think I'm the only one who thinks that of you."

"Are you afraid of me?"

"No." She definitely was not afraid of him.

"Do you hate me?"

"You just said you knew I would do anything for you. How can I hate you?"

"Because I'm a demanding boss, someone that everyone runs from as I walk through the room. Someone that people know I won't accept less than their very best. It would have to be hard to work for such a person." He laughed, although there wasn't much humor in it. "It is hard to work for such a person. I work for myself every day, and if you think I'm hard on other people, you should see how hard I am on myself."

"I've seen it. I know that you aren't half as hard on anyone else as you are on yourself."

"Thanks."

"It's the truth."

"So you're not scared of me, and you don't hate me." He paused, almost as though he wasn't sure how to phrase the next question. "What do you feel?"

Oh boy. She couldn't go there. She couldn't tell him. He was asking her to be vulnerable, when he hadn't been vulnerable himself. Except he had.

He had told her everything about his childhood. Stories he hadn't shared with anyone ever.

But...she couldn't just let him know.

She lifted her chin, then pushed herself off the floor, holding on to her carton as he released it at her sudden movement, then reaching with her other hand for his.

He handed it to her, and then he rose gracefully from the floor. She had to close her eyes and look away to keep from watching him. She always enjoyed the controlled way he moved. Like a jungle cat. Each move graceful, but containing power that was carefully leashed.

"You're not going to answer my question?"

"Yes. I'm going to answer. You told me more than you've ever told anyone else, to my knowledge anyway. How can I keep anything from you?"

"I didn't tell you that so that you would tell me what I wanted to know." He followed her to the garbage can, carrying the empty take-out bag. "It wasn't bribery or anything along those lines. Forget I even asked." Frustration lay in his tone as he threw the bag away. "Maybe I need to prove that I can be more than just about me. Maybe it's not about how you feel about me, but it's how I act toward you."

"What?" she asked, not understanding.

"I told you that I trusted you. Told you that more than anyone else, I know you will always make the decision that would be the best for me. You have my best interests at heart, and you will work for it. You don't know that about me. Not toward you. I've never once made a decision that was the best for you that caused me any hardship at all."

"You just flew home from the Cities for me. You stopped and got Chinese food. You brought it up. You knew I'd be working. You knew all those things about me, and you did that, even though it would have been easier for you to stay in the Cities."

"But I wanted to be here."

"Maybe I wanted to help you. Maybe I wanted to do those things because doing those things for you benefited me, since I work for you. I am part of your company. If good things happen in your company, good things happen to me, too. Right? How many times did I get a raise after I did something well? You compensated me for that."

"You can't buy loyalty."

"No. But you can't forget you were paying me. And I have never paid you a dime. Everything you've done for me has been because you wanted to, not because anyone was expecting you to or because your paycheck depended on it."

"Are you trying to tell me that the only reason you did anything good for me was because I was paying you? I'll call you a liar. And I know you're not one."

"No. You're right. I just didn't want to forget that. After all, money makes people do strange things sometimes."

"Tell me about it. That is truth."

"I like to eat." She smiled, hopefully breaking the tension. "That is truth, too."

"And I know it. That's why I came bearing peace offerings."

"You didn't have to come bearing anything. And you know that."

"Because it's my office."

"No. Not because of that. You know I'll always welcome you. Wherever I am."

"I really don't."

"You know it now."

She turned and wrapped her arms around herself. He had asked her a question, and she successfully changed the subject, and maybe he didn't remember that he asked, but later, he might remember she hadn't answered him, and she didn't want him to wonder or to think that she hadn't wanted to answer because there was some kind of negativity in her answer.

"You asked me how I felt about you."

"And I told you, you don't have to answer. I haven't done anything to prove myself to you."

"I've worked with you for seven years. I've worked with you rather closely for those seven years. I feel like I know you."

"You do."

"And I really like you. I really, really like you. More... More than the secretary should like her boss. That was before I even knew about your childhood. I admire what you've done with your life. I admire what you did this weekend. How you decided to make changes, and you didn't just think about those changes, but you started implementing them immediately, so much that I noticed the change."

"It's not a big deal."

"You can say that if you want to, but it takes a strength of character to decide you don't like the path you're on, even though it's a profitable one, and instead you're going to change directions. Especially for someone who's been as successful as you are. To give it all up. That means something."

"I suppose you're right."

"I know I am. And I admire you. I look up to you. And I...like you."

"And that right there made every second of the flight here and back, every bit of hassle, completely worth it." He grinned a little at her, and she returned it.

He didn't say anything more, although she kind of wished he would. Maybe he could say that they should have a relationship when he got to Strawberry Sands. They could work on building something. That maybe they would be good together. That he was interested in a romance that would lead to marriage and family... But he might not be marriage and family material. She'd suspected as much just knowing him for the last seven years, but after hearing his history, she would almost guarantee that's what he would say about himself. That he wasn't family material.

"How much more are you going to do in here tonight?" he asked as they turned back and looked at the office that was partially boxed up.

"I guess that's as good a place to quit as any. Honestly, it's harder for me to box up your office than it was mine or the break room. I... I just... You just seem to be a part of this. And I've struggled. That's why I kept it until last."

"It's just a building. Just an office. Just a place."

"The place where you've done a lot of business. A place where I grew a lot as a person. A place where I learned a lot. And you give yourself a hard time, but you were always very patient with me. I was scared to death of you in the first years, and you had to have known it, but you never gave me a hard time. Even when I spilled that coffee on you."

He barked out a laugh. "I totally forgot about that. And yeah, I knew it was because you were terrified. And I didn't mean to be so intimidating. I actually admired you, because even though you were scared, and I could tell it, you still smiled at me. You still greeted me like a friend. You still treated me like a human being, not like I was some kind of high-powered businessperson that didn't need someone to be friendly and nice to me."

She laughed a little. "I definitely thought you were some kind of high-powered businessperson. My dad used to say about people who thought they were really important, that they put their pants on one leg at a time just like he did. But I guess what I like to do is say to myself, God loves them too. They are God's child. God died for them. And that reminds me that in front of God, we're all on equal footing. You know?"

"Maybe that was the example I needed. And I must be a slow learner because I needed it for seven years before God finally got a hold of me."

She slanted a grin at him, and he smiled back at her, and for the first time, she felt like they were more equals than boss and subordinate, even though she wasn't confused about who gave the orders or who owned the company. It was just... He was her friend too. And she liked that.

<h1 style="text-align:center">Chapter 14</h1>

"Rodney? Are you awake?"

Rodney blinked in the darkness of his room. Of course he was awake. "Yeah?"

Becky was snuggled up next to him, lying on top of the covers, having grabbed the blanket that sat on the chair by the sliding glass doors that he always left unlocked now.

He knew she considered him like an older brother. And in some ways, he looked at her like a little sister. But in other ways, he knew very well that what they were doing could get him into a big pile of trouble. Huge trouble.

More trouble than he ever dreamed of being in, and certainly more trouble than he wanted.

But he felt like she needed him. And he liked that. Liked being needed. And liked...the sense that there was loyalty that lay between them.

He wasn't quite sure how his parents felt about him. Half the time, he thought they forgot he was even there until they wanted to parade him around some event or another.

"I'm going to quit."

It didn't register at first what she was saying. Then he tried to figure out what in the world she was talking about.

"Quit coming here?" He tried to keep his voice level and not show the panic that that thought involved. He would be better off if she did quit slipping into his room at night. He should encourage it.

"No. Dumbbell. Of course I would keep coming here. Where else would I sleep? Plus, I like you."

That was a pretty big admittance coming from Becky. Normally she didn't admit anything. Although, since she told him a little bit about her homelife, she'd opened up a bit more. He could say she was actually becoming affectionate with him. Which, on the one hand, he liked, on the other hand...he knew was even worse. But again, he liked her.

"Quit the farm."

"Your job?"

"I'll get a job somewhere else. I can't keep working there."

"Are they mean to you? Did you get hurt?" He stiffened and started to sit up.

She put a hand on his chest and said, "No."

He relaxed immediately. And without thinking about it, he put his hand over hers and pressed it closer.

He should let it go.

"The woman, Miss Kim, keeps insisting that I come into the house to eat. She wants to talk to me. She asked about my family. About where I live. She already tried to get my number and my address, and I gave her bogus stuff, and she figured it out. Now she's after me to get the right stuff. She wants to feed me, do whatever it is that do-gooders like her do. And you know as well as I do that I can't let her."

"Why not?" He spoke softly, quietly, almost as though if he spoke light enough, she wouldn't listen, wouldn't do it. After all, if she went to Kim, and Kim figured out about her situation, Becky would be going back to the state, and he'd lose her.

Plus, she'd be ripped from her sister, she'd be upset, she'd probably run away, and she might get hurt. Something could happen to her. He might not lose her just for a little bit, but he could lose her forever.

Without thinking, his arm tightened around her, and she snuggled closer to his side.

The blankets were between them, and that was a good thing.

"You know!" Becky said.

And immediately he said, "Shh! Do you want the whole house to hear you?"

"No. Of course not. But don't be stupid. If she finds out about me, the first thing she's going to do is call the cops, and I'll be riding in that patrol car going to jail!"

"You know you won't go to jail."

"I might as well be. You know what I meant. They're gonna take me and put me back in the system."

"You're still in the system. They just can't find you right now."

"Exactly. And that's exactly the way it needs to be. Otherwise, I'll be separated from Rita forever."

"They don't like to separate siblings. They place you close to her if they can."

"No one wants someone my age. A problem child. They think I'm going to slit their throats while they sleep or something."

"I guess you could get me to testify that you won't do that. I can do that if you need me to."

"Very funny."

"Come on. Why are you so serious? Lighten up a bit. Maybe going to Miss Kim will be the best thing that ever happened to you."

"How could that be? You know as well as I do that do-gooder conscience won't let her do anything except call the authorities. It might not be the cops, but you know it's going to be somebody, and you know they will take me away."

"Then maybe you'll find a good family."

"It's like you want to be rid of me, Dixie," she said, ripping her hand out from underneath his and flipping onto her back, although she stayed pressed close to his side. It was as though she needed him as much as he needed her.

"I've gotten used to having you around, Bekpet." He patted her shoulder awkwardly from where his arm lay underneath her. "We'll figure something out. I just don't think that going to the right people will be as bad as what you think it is."

For sure, if she went to his parents, they would definitely turn her in because they wouldn't want to be bothered with her. They would want to hand her over to someone else who would take care of her, and they wouldn't really give a flip about her sister or her family or her situation.

Rodney knew enough to know that not everyone thought the way his parents did. There were people who truly cared. There were people who knew that the law was the law but that sometimes the law wasn't the best way to go.

Or maybe the idea was that there were different ways to handle things.

Anyway, his gut told him that Kim and Davis, the people who owned the farm where Becky worked, would handle things differently.

"I thought you liked the horses."

"I do, Dixie. Haven't you been listening to me? I don't want to quit! I just have to." She said that last part softer. Sadly, like she really would miss her job.

"You told me that you love horses. That you want to grow up and be a horse trainer."

"Or something like that. I want to own a riding stable and rent horses out and get to work with them every single day. I want to take girls in. Girls that need homes, I want to give them good homes. With all of their siblings. And not just take one and not everyone."

Her voice cracked a little, and her body wobbled. Rodney figured she was probably biting back tears.

He would be. It would stink to have a sibling and have her be adopted out while the family didn't want him.

Of course, he would never know what that was like, because he was never going to get a sibling.

His parents probably felt like they made a mistake with the one child that they did have.

"Why don't you let me talk to them?"

"No!"

"Wasn't I right about the job to begin with?"

"That doesn't mean you're right about everything, Dixie."

"Why don't you trust me a little?"

"Because I don't trust anyone. There isn't anyone I've ever trusted that hasn't let me down."

"I haven't."

"You will. It's just a matter of time. I know."

She crossed her arms over her chest, and he could almost feel her staring at the ceiling.

He rolled over, facing her and tugging at her a little bit until she rolled onto her side and allowed him to spoon her through the covers.

"Come on. Admit it. You're wrong. There isn't anyone in the world that you can trust more than me."

"That might be true. But that doesn't mean that I can trust you any further than I can throw you, and considering that you weigh a ton, that's not saying much."

"All right. How about this. We'll go down tomorrow, or today rather, and I'll go with you. And I'll just nose around a little bit. And see what they think about things."

"No. I'm quitting, and that's final."

Rodney didn't say anything else. Becky could be as stubborn as anyone he'd ever met. She was like a brick wall when she made up her mind. But that was a good thing, too. Because when she gave her loyalty, she gave it with her whole heart. And for some reason, she was loyal to him.

He wasn't sure why, other than maybe he didn't tell on her and he fed her the first time he met her. She gave him access into her... Maybe not heart. But at least into her mind. Still, he knew there was no changing it this time. But he didn't need her permission. He could walk down with her whenever she went to work in the morning, and he could still talk. Whether she liked it or not.

It turned out that he fell asleep, and when he woke up, she was gone.

He grabbed his phone from his dresser and looked at the time. Eleven o'clock.

He hadn't gone to bed until after she had come in. Lately he'd been listening for her, watching and waiting.

He worried a little about what they were going to do when school started again. Becky needed a home. She couldn't just come into his house, sleep in his bed, and continue with what they were doing. Not only could he get in trouble, but it couldn't be good for her. As much as he...kind of wanted to keep it the way it was.

He went to the kitchen to grab one of the pastries that were usually sitting on the counter. His mom hated it, because it wasn't healthy, but his dad always kept some goodies around and just laughed at his mom's irritation.

He was pretty sure his parents weren't sharing the same room anymore, but he tried to stay out of their business, because he didn't like to know those kinds of things.

He could hear his mom talking on a conference call through the door to her room, and he could also hear his dad's music blasting from his dad's office door.

Neither one of them were going to notice if he was gone. He didn't bother to tell them.

There was nothing on the schedule for him to do today, nothing until next week when he had tennis lessons at the country club in Blueberry Beach.

He could leave until then, and he was pretty sure his parents wouldn't notice. Giving Karen, who worked in the kitchen, a wink, he waved the pastry he snatched from the carton on the counter and walked by her.

She clucked her tongue at him, shaking her head, but didn't say anything.

Chapter 15

Rodney walked back to his room, grabbed his wallet, shoved it in his back pocket, and walked down over the fields toward Strawberry Sands. After a few miles, he hit the upper end, intending to walk through town to the stable on the far side. He was late enough that Becky might even be done with her work. If so, she might be at the diner. He'd peek in on his way by.

Turned out he didn't have to, since she came up the sidewalk as he walked down.

He nodded at one of the Landry brothers, Luke he thought it was, who was hauling a load of hay through town. He pretended not to see Kristin and her gram, Miss Heather, as they came out of the diner and headed across the street.

Miss Heather was a force of nature. He almost thought that she was probably a lot like Becky when she was little. He told that to Becky once, that she was going to grow up and be just like Miss Heather, and Becky had gotten so mad at him she hadn't talked to him for a week.

It wasn't his fault she couldn't handle the truth.

He laughed a little at the thought.

As he walked by the diner, he glanced in, seeing Miss Chi standing at a table, laughing with the patron. The patron had his hand on her hip, and it slid down around her thigh.

Rodney wrinkled his nose. He knew plenty of people like that from the circles his parents moved in. He wouldn't have thought Chi was a person like that, though. She moved just slightly, and the man's hand fell off. Maybe she hadn't wanted it there.

But when she moved, he got a better look at the man and his heart stopped. Then it started to beat harder, like he'd run the whole way from his house to the diner, instead of walking.

That man was his dad.

Hundreds of thoughts ran through his head, thousands, in just seconds. There had been music blasting from his dad's door. Was that a ruse? His mom hated it, and she stayed far away from it. Did his dad want her to stay away while he was gone, so he left the music playing?

Funny, but the thought that circulated over and over was the fact that his parents had said, both of them, over and over, that Strawberry Sands was just a hick town, with nothing to recommend it, and they never went there. They enjoyed their house on the bluffs, the big ocean view, and all that came with it, but Blueberry Beach was where they called home.

They didn't like to admit that they were from such a tiny, nowhere town, and to hear his dad talk, the place was basically a ghost town.

But there he was, sitting in the diner, his hand just having been brushed off the waitress's thigh.

Rodney turned sharply, doing a complete one hundred eighty and rushing to the path that ran between the diner and the building beside it.

Halfway back, he leaned against the cool wood of the wall, putting his head back and closing his eyes, trying to still the staccato beating of his heart.

It didn't mean anything. Didn't mean anything but his dad had wandering hands.

It didn't mean his dad was cheating. Didn't mean he was thinking about it. Didn't mean anything.

Except it did.

Anyone knew that a married man should not touch another woman's thigh.

He never even saw his dad touch his mom's thigh. In fact, thinking back over the last year, he couldn't remember his dad touching his mom at all. Nor her him.

And yet there was his dad, laughing and touching the waitress.

The music was a ruse. A cover.

Rodney gritted his teeth. His dad was a fraud.

"Dixie. Why did you run from me? Are you ashamed of me?"

Becky's shrill voice cut through the clutter in his head, and he straightened away from the wall.

"Why would I run from you, Bekpet? And why would I be ashamed of you?" They'd been in the diner before. Although both of them knew they had to be careful. People might think they were brother and sister, but if they saw them too often, they'd want to know where they were from, where they lived, where their parents were, and all kinds of other things that small towns were notoriously nosy about.

"Did you just get up?" Becky narrowed her eyes and looked at him. For a girl as young as she was, she was pretty shrewd.

He swallowed. He didn't want her to know anything. He couldn't let her know what a mess his family was.

Then he almost laughed. Her family was a bigger mess than his.

Still, it was a pride thing, he just couldn't admit that anything was less than perfect. Even though it was far, far less than perfect.

He had no proof. No proof at all. Just because his dad touched someone inappropriately didn't mean that he did all the time.

He just needed time to process. Time to think. Time to rationalize.

"Did you quit?" he asked, suddenly remembering his early morning conversation with Becky.

"No." She looked down at the ground, digging a toe into the dirt. "She wouldn't let me."

He laughed. "She wouldn't let you? Did you find someone who is more stubborn than what you are? I think I need to meet this woman."

"Shut up, Dixie."

"Didn't anyone ever tell you that it's not nice to say shut up?"

"I can say a lot of other words that would make your ears turn purple and fall off," Becky said, sticking her nose up in the air at him and treating him like he was two instead of six years older than she was.

"Why don't you take me to see your sister?" he said suddenly, not wanting to go in the diner and eat. Even though the pastry that he'd had on the way hadn't even come close to filling him up.

"No. Miss Kim made me go and sit down at her table and eat." Becky said it like it was the worst thing that had ever happened to her.

"Oh, you poor thing. She made you eat. She probably said you're skin and bones, and it was probably delicious." Miss Kim looked like someone who knew how to cook.

"She asked me to hold her baby." Becky said that a little bit more slowly, and it made Rodney notice. It meant something to Becky.

He peered at her.

"She trusted you with her baby?" he said, and there was no sarcasm in his voice. This was important to her.

"She did. How could I quit after that?"

"You couldn't." He knew sure as he was standing there that Kim had probably earned Becky's undying loyalty with that one small gesture. Trusting her with a tiny life that was the most important thing in the world to Miss Kim. Giving it to Becky to hold. Becky wouldn't take that lightly. Rodney knew that for sure. He loved that about Becky too. How fiercely loyal she was. How tough she acted, but how sensitive she actually was on the inside.

"Becky!" a voice said, startling Rodney. For some reason, he had the urge to run. Probably because for some reason, he had been sure it was going to be his dad coming around the corner of the building, and Rodney hadn't figured out how he was going to handle the new information.

It could be nothing. He tried to convince himself of that.

"Yes, ma'am," Becky said, straightening, with the cloud coming over her face that always seemed to surround her when she was dealing with adults. Like she couldn't be her true self.

Rodney was cognizant enough to know that she was too little to be so hard.

But he didn't know what to do about it. Other than be the kind of friend that she could always depend on. As much as he could anyway.

Even though he felt like his own world had been shifted in a very deep and disastrous way.

"I'm so glad that was you. I was pretty sure I saw you disappearing around the corner of the diner."

Rodney recognized Clara, one of the Landry kids. Mrs. Landry owned the bed-and-breakfast on the edge of town, and her kids owned and worked on the farm. Except for Clara, who worked for some bigwig in Chicago. But she was normally around on the weekends. Being that today was Saturday, it shouldn't be a shock to see her. Rodney figured he was just jumpy.

She didn't wait for Becky to say anything but kept talking, holding up the casserole dish in her hand.

"I hope you were on your way to work at Davis and Kim's. And I was wondering if you could take this down to them. They have all the ingredients to make the breakfast casserole in this dish, and Griff wanted to send it on down, since Kim had asked for the recipe." Clara grinned. "It's just like Griff to go over and above what anyone would be expected to do and not just give her the recipe but all the ingredients as well. That's Griff." She shook her head with a fun smile on her face.

Everyone in town loved Griff. Even though he did look rather scary and didn't always talk a whole lot. Rodney was coming to believe that he was one of the nicest people in town. He also overheard all the gossip about Griff having a thing for the diner owner.

That was too bad, because she seemed to not even notice that he was alive. He did so much for her, and she really didn't appreciate it at all.

Becky didn't mention to Clara that she had already been to the farm and completed her work.

That didn't surprise Rodney. Becky acted all tough and everything, but she really just wanted someone to love her.

Rodney could see under her gruff and tough exterior to the softy that was underneath. Maybe it was the nights that they'd spent together where she curled up next to him, as though she wanted to borrow from his strength and presence.

Not that he felt strong in any way.

Becky straightened and held her hands out for the container. "I'll make sure Miss Kim gets this."

Clara smiled and looked relieved. "Thank you so much. I know Kim wanted it, and I just have so many things to do today. I really appreciate your help."

Her words made Becky's shoulders push back, and the expression on her face shifted just slightly to make her look pleased and happy.

Clara turned and walked away, and then Becky lifted her brows at Rodney. "Are you coming?"

He almost said yes. He wanted to go somewhere, but he didn't want to be around people right now. "You go on ahead. Some of us have things we need to do. You know, because we have families and all that."

It was a low blow, but somehow he was hurting inside, and he just wanted to lash out at the world.

He felt bad immediately when Becky's face, rather than looking hurt, closed, like a shield had come down over the front of it.

"I'm sorry. That was mean. I... I just have a couple things I need to work out. I didn't mean to say something so unkind to you."

He didn't typically apologize. His dad had taught him that it was wrong.

But it worked. Becky's face didn't exactly return to the open, trusting look she had just a few seconds ago, but the force field-like impassiveness dissipated.

"That's fine. I was already there, but I can't believe she's trusting me to do this all by myself. Like... Like I'm part of the town. You know?"

Rodney nodded. He understood what she was saying. He felt like an outsider too. Maybe because his parents weren't part of the town, and people didn't really know him. He felt like he needed to protect himself from their prying eyes and ears.

Becky probably felt the same way. Like she couldn't quite trust them.

"Maybe I'll see you around."

"It's Saturday. I thought we would hang out on the beach or something."

"Aren't you going to go see your sister?"

"She won't be up until at least dinnertime."

"It's almost that time now."

"Maybe that's where I'll go when I'm done taking this to Miss Kim."

He nodded and then jerked his head. "Better get going."

Her eyes narrowed at him, like she was wondering what he might be hiding, but maybe it was the stuff in her hands that pushed her on, knowing she needed to do her duty and be responsible with what someone had entrusted her with.

Rodney smiled a little at the proud lift of her shoulders as she walked off, out from between the buildings and starting down the sidewalk.

He almost watched her until she disappeared from sight, but he got back between the buildings, intent on being alone. He needed to figure out this shift in his world and what he was going to do about it.

Chapter 16

Becky almost whistled as she walked down the sidewalk. Kim had entrusted her with holding the baby today, and now someone else in town, someone she didn't even work for, had given her an entire pan of food and asked her to deliver it. It was like they didn't even think that she was going to steal it or anything.

It was a new sensation. She wasn't used to being trusted. She wasn't used to being treated like she was worth something and wasn't a nuisance.

She liked it. If only she could get her own house and live by herself. She might only be twelve, but she was good at taking care of herself. And while she had been planning on quitting her job earlier, somehow, just the act of Miss Clara giving her the casserole and entrusting her to carry it made her feel like...maybe she wouldn't. She just had to be able to evade the questions that Miss Kim kept wanting to ask. But so far, she had been successful. Maybe she could continue to dodge them.

She allowed her natural optimism to take over, figuring that the street smarts that she picked up would carry her through. They always had before. So far anyway. She managed to be in the same town as her sister and see her almost every day. She might even manage to figure out how to go to school.

She kind of felt like that was important. Everyone said that a kid needed education in order to be successful. She wasn't entirely sure about that, but it couldn't hurt to hedge her bets.

It was a beautiful, sunny day, and she nodded at several people she passed on the sidewalk as she headed toward Miss Kim's.

The horses were already out, and many of them were in the pasture. She loved the way that looked, with the horses in the field, the wind stirring their manes and tails and the lake in the distance. She wasn't sure there was anything more beautiful in the world, and when she grew up, she wanted a place just like this.

As she looked closer, she saw a figure standing, rather than leaning on the fence. It didn't take long to recognize Miss Kim.

The car seat sat beside her, and Becky didn't hear anything, so she figured the baby was sleeping.

Although, now that she was closer, she did hear something. Something that sounded like crying, but not a baby.

Miss Kim's shoulders shook in time to the sounds Becky heard, and she realized it was Miss Kim. She was crying.

Becky didn't know what to do. Her first instinct was to turn around and run. She didn't think that any adult she knew would ever want to be caught crying; it would probably make them mad. And Becky would be the one they would yell at.

Even though she didn't think she was doing anything wrong. She promised that she would deliver the ingredients in the pan. She had to do it. But should she just slip into the house, walking right by Miss Kim?

Miss Kim had been concerned about her. She'd been nosy, yes, and asked way too many questions and made Becky nervous, but she still was doing it because she was kind and caring.

Becky had never really met anyone who truly, truly cared about her. Not the way Miss Kim did.

And that was just since she brought the baby home from the hospital. It hadn't been long, and from what Becky understood, the baby had a lot of problems and Miss Kim should be focused on that. But instead, she'd given some of her time and energy to take care of Becky.

That last thought was what did it for Becky. She changed her direction so she swerved off the drive and into the grass, slowing down until she almost crept up on Miss Kim.

She took a deep breath and said a tiny prayer that Miss Kim wouldn't be mad at her. "Miss Kim?"

Just like Becky thought, Miss Kim jumped as though startled.

"You scared me!" she said, her hand going to her chest. "I didn't think anyone was out here." She swiped hastily at the tear tracks on her cheeks.

"Are you okay?" Becky asked, even though she knew it wasn't any of her business.

"I'm fine," she said. "Mostly." She smiled a little. "I just heard from my oldest daughter. Alyssa." Miss Kim sniffed, and her eyes filled again.

Becky waited.

"I've tried so hard. Did the very best I could. I mean... I think it was the divorce that threw her over the edge, but I couldn't help it. There wasn't anything I could do. It wasn't like I was the one who cheated. I wasn't the one who left either. And honestly, if he had wanted to get back together, if he had apologized and tried to make things right, I would have done it. For Alyssa."

Becky didn't think that Miss Kim was really talking to her. But she just stood quiet and allowed her to talk.

"And now Alyssa has gone so far away from me, I don't know what to do to reach her. She just... She just seems like a different person than the kid I raised. I still love her so much."

She closed her mouth and looked up to the sky like there were answers there before she seemed to get a hold of herself and remembered that Becky was still standing there.

"What do you have?" she asked, nodding at the container in Becky's hands.

"Miss Clara said that Mr. Griff said you wanted the recipe, and so he gave you the recipe, but he also gave you everything that you needed in order to make it."

"Everything?" Miss Kim asked, surprise in her voice as she walked closer to Becky and looked at the stuff in her hands.

"Yep. That's what Miss Clara said."

"Oh my goodness," Miss Kim said, her hand going to her throat. "I can't believe the generosity of the people in this town."

"I heard it's really good," Becky offered, not really knowing what else to say but unspeakably relieved now that Miss Kim wasn't crying anymore.

"Oh, it is! Haven't you ever had a breakfast casserole?" Miss Kim almost seemed like herself again.

"No."

"What are you doing today? Would you like to come into the kitchen and make it with me? We'll cook it, and then we'll eat. I bet Davis will really appreciate having a nice lunch like that. It's more than he was expecting today, I'm sure." She gave Becky a little smile. "He's working with Matt and Luke on their farm today. I'll have enough here for everyone. I'm going to text Miss Lana and let her know that I'll provide lunch today."

"I bet she'll appreciate that. I heard the bed-and-breakfast was really busy."

"You really get around," Kim said as her fingers flew over her phone.

When a person didn't have a house, they had a tendency to get around, but Becky didn't mention that, of course.

True to her word, Miss Kim picked up the car seat, where Kathleen continued to sleep soundly, and walked back to the house with Becky.

Becky had never cooked anything from a recipe, nothing that didn't come from a box, and so putting the tater tots and the eggs and the cheese all together was a new experience for her. Miss Kim almost felt like...a mother, as she patiently allowed Becky to crack eggs and explained each step as they did it.

Becky figured she probably couldn't make it again, but if she did this a few more times, she could cook for herself. That dream of owning her own home might be a reality sooner than she thought.

"So you did tell me where you lived, but the address you gave me wasn't an actual address," Kim said in a conversational tone as they cleaned up the counters. The casserole was in the oven baking, and Becky's stomach growled. Still, she was tempted to make a quick getaway. Because she didn't want to talk about her home or her lack of it.

"My little sister lives with the family at the end of town." She rattled off their name. That was more than she ever told anyone, and maybe she was wrong to be trusting Miss Kim.

"Your little sister lives with..." Kim was in the process of wringing out the rag she had used to wipe the counter slowly, and her movements were even slower as she turned the water off. "Your little sister lives with them. But you don't?"

"No. When you're in the foster system, you have a tendency to get split up." She felt a little bit of an affinity with Miss Kim. After all, Miss Kim would understand how it felt to have your family ripped away. After her tears over Alyssa, Becky thought that she probably could understand Becky's pain.

"So you're in the foster care system," Miss Kim said, in that slow, thoughtful way as though she were processing things.

Becky nodded, scrubbing the measuring cup in the sink before rinsing it off and setting it in the drainboard.

"So you don't live with your biological parents, you live with foster parents."

Becky didn't want to lie. She'd lied enough over her life, and Rodney had told her how terrible lying was. That was some of the things that they talked about late at night when she popped into his room. He wasn't super religious, but he had a code of ethics. A code of ethics because of his parents not having any code of ethics. That's what he said anyway.

So, Becky didn't say anything. There was no way for her to answer that question without lying.

"Becky. You know you can trust me, right?"

"I understood why you were crying over your daughter. That made sense to me. Because the most important thing to me in the world is to be with my sister. She's the only family I have."

"Right. Your sister is important to you the way Alyssa is important to me." Kim paused. "And you would do anything for her."

Becky nodded.

"Even run away."

Becky's eyes widened. She wasn't going to tell her, but... What was she going to do now?

"If I had, would you turn me in?" Not that she ever trusted adults. They lied constantly. She didn't feel like she had much choice.

"I think I would get in trouble if I didn't. But...maybe it will be possible that I can provide a place for you to live so you could see your sister. Would that sound like something you would be interested in?" Her voice sounded completely unsure, like she was throwing something out way in the left field, and she wasn't sure how Becky would respond to it.

"Provide a place to live? Like... I could live in the stable with the horses?" That would be awesome. That would be better than anything she could ever think of. If she were allowed to stay in Strawberry Sands, if she were allowed to stay in the stable, if she didn't have to leave every morning. If...maybe she could talk Kim into letting her help with the baby, or help cook, or help with something, where she could eat too. It wouldn't be her own house, but she could save up to buy her own house. Eventually. Maybe when she was fourteen or something.

"Or... You could live in the house with Davis and me and Kathleen."

Becky stopped, her head swiveled to Miss Kim, and her eyes opened wide, as wide as they could possibly go. "Live here?"

"Would you be interested?"

"I couldn't. There's no way. Somebody would find me, and you guys would get in trouble. And I don't want you guys to get in trouble. You've already been so nice to me." Her voice kept rising the longer she spoke, and she spoke faster because she was so upset, because even though Miss Kim had just given her the very best thing that she could possibly ever give her, she couldn't take her up on it. Because she didn't want Miss Kim to get in trouble.

"No. I would make sure that was okay. We'd go through all the proper channels, and we would make sure that everything was the way it should be." Kim stopped talking and stared at her thoughtfully. "Unless there's someone else you'd rather live with?"

Becky stopped. She wanted to live with Rodney. But his parents would never be okay with that. She loved Miss Kim, and she'd be happy with Miss Kim and Mr. Davis, but they had Kathleen. And they probably wouldn't be willing to adopt her sister.

"I think... I'd like to live with someone who doesn't have any children already."

If Miss Kim were really going to help her, which she had her doubts about, she wanted to be honest.

There was hurt on Miss Kim's face, and she felt bad about that, but it was the truth.

Still, it made her mouth move. "I love the horses. I love feeding them. I love working there. I want to have a barn of my own someday."

"I'm sure you will," Miss Kim said.

"But... You already have Alyssa and also Kathleen. And I have my sister. She... She's not in a great place. I mean, they feed her, and they keep it warm in the winter. But they're not very nice to her. She's just money, you know?"

Miss Kim blinked, as though she had never considered that foster kids could just be money.

"Foster parents get paid for helping foster kids. That's what my sister is to this family."

"Oh, I think there's a lot of work involved. Surely the money they get isn't worth all the work they have to do."

"To some people, it is. Especially if they can cut corners with the kids. Anyway, maybe, maybe not. But she's not really happy there. She wants to be with me the same as I want to be with her."

"You just need someone who will take two children?"

"And I'm too old. Nobody wants me. She is only five, and she's cute. Anybody will take her. It's me that's the problem."

That was the truth. As much as it hurt to say it, and she didn't really understand, although she supposed she really did. She knew foster kids who, if given half a chance, really would slit someone's throat while they slept. It seemed to be what all foster parents thought about teenage foster kids.

"Can I think about this for a little bit?" Miss Kim said as the buzzer on the stove went off, indicating that the casserole was finished. It made Miss Kim smile, and she said, "But in the meantime, we can eat, right? And we'll take Kathleen, and we'll deliver some to the guys so they have some lunch."

"We get to eat?" Becky said, wondering if Miss Kim was mad at her now that she said she didn't want to live with her. She was just being honest. But maybe Rodney wasn't right, and honesty wasn't always the best policy.

"Of course. We'll get some out for ourselves and leave it on the counter to cool while we deliver the casserole and some plates to the guys. I have a jug I can fill up with water, and we'll grab some cups, too. While we're doing that, we'll think about this. I think it's a good thing to pray about as well." Kim pursed her lips. "In the meantime, I'll have to talk to Davis, but maybe it would be okay for you to stay here. Where have you been staying?"

"Around," Becky said, not wanting to give the name of Rodney or his parents. Rodney had been a little bit afraid that he would get in trouble, and she thought he might be right. She didn't want to implicate him in any way.

"All right. Maybe we can figure out where around is, but in the meantime, no one's going to miss you if you stay here?"

"No." She would be sure to tell Rodney what was going on. He would be the only one who would be concerned about her. And maybe she was flattering herself, but she thought he actually really liked her, and he truly would be worried.

Becky nodded. She supposed in her own way, she prayed about it some. But it was hard to believe in a God who allowed her to be separated from the only family she had.

God, if You get my sister and I back together so that we live under the same roof, I might just start believing in You again.

Chapter 17

"It's strange to see you here on a Monday," Kristin said as Clara walked down the sidewalk early Monday morning. The sun wasn't quite up, but Kristin was already out walking three little dogs on leashes.

Clara smiled at the antics of the little animals. She was pretty sure one of the dogs belonged to Miss Heather. The others probably belonged to Miss Heather's friends. Funny that Kristen was the one walking them.

"Well, actually, my schedule shifted."

"Really? You mean you quit your job?" Kristin smiled. "You've been thinking about that for a while."

"Well, that's not exactly what happened." They walked slowly along the sidewalk, until it ended at the sand dunes, and then they continued on toward the beach. "My boss decided that he wanted to move his headquarters to Strawberry Sands, and he bought the schoolhouse last week."

"He bought the schoolhouse? I didn't even hear about that? How… That was fast."

"Yeah. I don't know whether where he's from has anything to do with it or not, but he has the connections to make things happen." Clara still couldn't believe that it had actually gone through. The moving trucks were coming the next day, so… "I have today off. He has to get a hold of some contractors, but he's going to do a lot of the interior renovations himself."

"Your big-city Chicago boss is going to do the renovations himself?"

Clara laughed at the incredulity in Kristin's tone.

"I know, right? Who would have thought. But... He's changed in just the last week or so." Clara didn't know whether she could go into all the things that had factored into his change. She wasn't sure herself that she believed it was a permanent thing. A lot of times, people tried something new, found it didn't work for them, and went back to what they were doing before.

She had thought that that might be what was going to happen with Alex. Except Alex wasn't the kind of man who started on a path and didn't finish what he started. He certainly couldn't have been as successful as what he was if that were the kind of thing that he did.

"That's a pretty big change. He's moving from Chicago to Strawberry Sands and fixing up an old abandoned schoolhouse to turn into his office? Did he fall and hit his head? Have a cancer diagnosis? Survive an earthquake?"

Clara laughed. "It is pretty unbelievable, isn't it?"

"Never mind. He fell in love, didn't he?" Kristin's tone was softer; although there was a little bit of teasing there, there was a lot of hope and happiness too.

"No. I don't think so. Not with me anyway." If that's what she was trying to say.

"Well, kinda sounds like he has. Either that or he had a come-to-Jesus moment."

"Now that might have happened. He was here last weekend. He went to church. You saw him?" She couldn't remember whether she had seen Kristin at church or not.

"Yeah. The tall, dark, quiet guy that was beside you. He kind of looked like he was glowering at everything, and I got the feeling you forced him to come."

"I did not. He came on his own, and he actually listened. Not only that, but he did things that most people don't—he listened, and then he put what he heard into practice. Immediately." She wouldn't expect Alex to do anything else. He wasn't a wait around and see kind of guy.

"Wow. That's a lot of changes to make in a week."

"Yeah. So I've been thinking about quitting my job because he wanted me to move to the Cities. But now, he spent the week canceling that and planning the move here."

"That's a major change."

"Isn't that what we're supposed to do when we become Christians though? Our whole lives are supposed to take a shift. It's not like we pick up Jesus, like a suitcase, and carry him along wherever we're going. It's like... Like we turn from the way that we were going and turn toward Jesus, willing to do whatever he wants us to do. Isn't that true conversion?"

"Repentance means to turn away. We're supposed to turn away from sin. I don't know that we're necessarily supposed to turn away from our lives though."

"If they're not lives that glorify the Lord, we should. Although, I think even Christians have ways of living that are totally for themselves and not for God. Maybe that's what revival is. Turning away from the paths that we're on, that have been leading us away from God, and moving back closer to Him. Rededicating our lives to Him."

"Wow. So maybe your boss will start a revival in Strawberry Sands?"

Clara laughed. If someone had told her that two weeks ago, she would have thought that was the funniest thing she ever heard. But it was convicting when a person saw someone who met Jesus and made true, sincere changes in their lives. It convicted that person that maybe that's what they should be doing too.

"Last week in church though, I told you that he was quiet and a little scary, but... There was a way that he looked at you. I guess that's why I thought maybe you forced him to go to church. It was just the way he looked when he looked at you. Like..." Kristin laughed a little, tugging on the lead to keep the dogs from getting all tangled. "Like he would do anything for you. That he admires you that much. Just something."

Clara took one of the leashes from Kristin to keep the dogs from getting tangled, and Kristin thanked her.

Clara didn't know what to say to what Kristen had just told her.

"I like him. I can't deny it. In fact..." She looked around, then lowered her voice. "I've had a crush on him forever. That was part of the reason that I was ever considering going to the Cities. Because the idea of not being around him again was...depressing. But I didn't think it would go anywhere. And now, not only am I not moving to the Cities, but he came here."

"And you're still going to be working for him?"

"I'm not sure. I haven't given any notice yet. But after the Strawberry Festival, I kinda thought that maybe I'd want to start my own shop. There are a couple of empty buildings along Main Street, and while I know it wouldn't make me a ton of money, he gave me fifty thousand for everything in my tent. That's a nice bit of seed money."

"He bought everything in your tent at the festival?" Kristin said, her voice sounding shrill in her surprise.

Clara looked around again. The beach was deserted; the sun wasn't even up yet. Although it was getting lighter by the second.

"He did. But I think it was more because he wanted to go eat, and he didn't want to wait around while I sold everything else."

"He could have gone to eat by himself, Clara. That man. I think that man...may be in love with you."

Chapter 18

Alex backed the trailer up next to the schoolhouse and shut the truck off.

He'd been working all morning inside with a crowbar, taking out the flooring and the walls that he knew were going to need to go. He'd already decided that he wanted Clara to have an office facing the lake. Something with windows, where she could set up an easel and do her painting.

He hadn't quite reconciled in his mind exactly how she was going to work for him and paint at the same time, but it was important that she was able to do the art she was born to do.

He was covered in dust and dirt and realized as he got out of the truck that he was starving.

He walked around, going toward the front of the school, figuring he'd look at the view for just a few minutes and try to get his brain settled down. He had a hundred things he wanted to do, plans he'd already made, and more he needed to make. Plus, leaving the business that he'd been in wasn't just a snap of his fingers and have it done. He was still tying up loose ends from that too.

As he looked out over the lake, he realized there were three men walking up the hill through the dunes in the sparse grass.

He looked over toward the pasture where Clara's family kept their horses.

He wasn't sure why, other than he thought that they looked like her brothers. The two that he knew anyway. Matt, whom he'd seen several times, and... Luke maybe.

He hoped they weren't coming up because they had heard what he was doing and were upset about it.

Small towns tended to be like that. They didn't like to change anything. For some reason, he felt driven to move ahead. Maybe it was because of his fear of losing Clara, but he didn't think that was it. He just...knew this was what the Lord wanted him to do, and he wasn't the kind of man who sat around on things.

God knew that. Although there had been definite times in his life where God had told him to calm down and have patience.

Thankfully, this didn't seem to be one of those times, even if things weren't progressing as fast as he would like between Clara and him. She...was resistant to the idea of them moving forward in their relationship, or maybe she hadn't understood the hints that he'd been dropping.

Maybe he wasn't as bold as what he needed to be. Or maybe she just needed time to shift gears in her mind as to how things would change down the road.

He hoped that was it. Hoped that she saw a little bit of something in him that she might want to spend more time with. A lot more time, since he was looking at the rest of their lives.

"Hey there," Matt said as they crested the hill and walked the rest of the distance over the old, cracked blacktop in front of the school. Weeds grew up through the cracks, but it would still work as a parking area. Not that he was parking anything there. The only people he planned to have working in the offices were Clara and himself.

"Hey. Nice day for a walk," he said, grinning a bit.

"It is, although we were working just down the beach, and we knew you were up here, and we thought maybe you might be interested in joining us for lunch?" The men finally stopped in front of him, and he nodded.

"This is my brother Luke. I know you've met him. And then you know Davis who lives up the beach and owns the horses right here."

Alex shook both of their hands. "Nice to meet you," he said, liking the honest and upright look in both men's eyes, their firm handshakes, and the way they seemed casually at ease.

"Always good to have a great neighbor," Davis said. "I heard you were moving in."

"I am. That's true. I'm making some offices, and I'm going to live in the other side."

"Every time I go in town, people ask me why you didn't buy the big house on the beach. Like I would know," Luke said with a grin. But there were questions in his eyes.

"You want the honest answer?" Alex asked, figuring he could be straight with these men. Maybe he would have tried to give someone else the runaround, not lying, just...not telling the truth.

"Yeah. What other kind of answer is there?" Luke asked, like people didn't lie on a daily basis. Maybe around here they didn't. Although Alex doubted it. Mankind was the same whether they were in a big town or small. Still, maybe there were more people to hold a person accountable in a small town. In the city, family and friends often didn't have any idea what a person was doing, and they didn't have a sense of community that they would be held responsible to.

"This is what Clara wanted."

That was as simple as it got.

He didn't move, letting his hands hang at his sides. Aware that he had just said that to Clara's brothers.

"I think she misjudged you," Luke said, smirking.

"In what way?" Although he was pretty sure he knew. He'd already heard that Clara said he was an intimidating boss. A hard driver.

He shook his head when Luke looked uncomfortable.

"Never mind. She probably said something like I was demanding and maybe a little bit scary and intimidating. And none of those things would be untrue. But..." He was a little uncomfortable just saying it, but again, the truth was the truth. "I was in church last week, and I realized a lot of things that I should have been doing but haven't been. I decided I was going to make some changes, not the least of which was to stop trusting in myself and start trusting in Jesus. I guess that would be the first thing, but I suppose that all three of you know that when you do that, life has a tendency to change."

"It should. But a lot of times, it doesn't," Luke said easily.

"I'm glad to hear it. Actually, I'm really glad to hear it," Matt said thoughtfully. Then, a grin broke across his face. "So Clara wanted the schoolhouse?"

There was a little bit of insinuation in those words, and Alex didn't have any trouble hearing it.

"She did. She... She was the reason I was in church. And I've never worked with anyone I enjoy working with more. I suppose the idea that she might not stay with me, and that she might be opening up a shop of her own, prompted me to make some changes. Which forced me to recognize the fact that I wasn't really living like I should be."

"How about we sit down and talk about it. That food smells really good," Luke said, pointing to the casserole that Davis carried with the plates he held in his hand.

"Mind if we join you?" Matt said again.

"Sure. I don't know how sturdy that picnic table is. It looks like it's been here since before the war, but we can try it. Nice views anyway."

"I don't know about the war, but it's been there since I went to school here anyway," Luke said good-naturedly as they started toward the table Alex had indicated.

"It's pretty sturdy. Just don't slide across the board, you might get a splinter in your butt, and I'm not taking it out for you," Matt said, looking at what Alex assumed to be his little brother. Even though Luke was taller than Matt.

"I think my wife would get any splinters out that I got, but I'm not sure she'd appreciate it, so I think I'll be careful. Thanks for the warning," Davis said, setting the casserole down on the table.

Matt set down the cooler he carried along with the cups, and before long, they had the plates out, the food dished, and Luke had said the blessing.

"You haven't seen a little girl running around here anywhere, have you?" Davis said casually after they talked about the weather and a few other things that were happening in town. The Harvest Festival being one. Which had Alex wanting to roll his eyes at how small towns loved their festivals.

"No. Did someone lose a child?" Alex asked, surprised that he hadn't heard as much from Clara. In fact, he hadn't heard anything from her all day. He'd told her to take Monday off, and since he hadn't been in town, he hadn't seen her.

He had to admit there was a small part of him that hoped she would come up, if not to see him, at least to see the school. He just wanted to...talk to her for a few minutes. Funny how when she was gone, he missed her like that.

"Not really. My wife just said the little girl that's been helping us with the stable—she must be twelve or fourteen or something like that—admitted to her today that her sister is in foster care here in Strawberry Sands, and the older girl ran away from her foster home so that she could be with her sister. My wife got the impression that she is...homeless."

"The little girl that works in the stable? Becky?" Matt said, knowing immediately who Davis was talking about.

"Yeah. Becky."

"What about the boy that's with her?"

"I didn't think to ask about him. I assumed that was her brother. Or maybe she told me it was. Honestly, with Kathleen being in the NICU, that's where all of my focus was, and I was just thrilled to have dependable people helping me with the horses. I didn't think to question her too much. Of course, my wife has different instincts, and ever since we brought Kathleen home, she's been worrying this question in her mind, where the little girl is from, where her parents are, and what's going on with her." Davis shrugged, like he couldn't help it that he'd missed all of that.

"So you think the little girl has been just hanging out in town? Living nowhere? Where is she sleeping?" Alex asked, thinking back to his own childhood. He'd been neglected, sure. But he'd always had a home.

"I'm not sure. I don't think she knows either."

"I've seen her at the diner. Maybe she's taking the money that she's earning there and buying food for herself at the diner." Luke lifted his shoulder, sticking a forkful of food in his mouth.

"Should we find her and give her something to eat?" Alex asked, more concerned than he liked to admit.

"My wife is feeding her now. She had to use the restroom, and my wife called me, just to clue me in on what was going on. She asked if I could make some discreet inquiries. The little girl was very concerned that the authorities were going to come and take her away and she wouldn't be able to see her sister anymore. My wife didn't want that to happen, because Becky isn't the kind of person who trusts very easily, and Kim didn't want her to get stabbed in the back."

"You guys should adopt her," Matt said easily, his eyes following one of the horses as it lifted its head, then galloped across the field and down over the hill.

Alex watched the horse too, remembering that horses made up a good portion of the paintings that Clara had drawn. Maybe that was another reason why she liked the school better than she liked the fancy new house.

"Kim offered. At least offered to let her live there, but the girl said that Kim had the baby and Alyssa, and she didn't think taking in two more girls would be something Kim would want to do."

"But her sister already has a home," Luke pointed out.

"I think Becky is hoping that her sister will eventually live with her. I'm sure that's what she wants. Kim said something about her saying that she was unadoptable because she was so old. I guess most couples don't want to start out with a teenager."

"That's smart," Alex murmured. He was a handful when he was a teenager. If it hadn't been for his uncle, he probably would have gone off the deep end. He owed his uncle more than he could repay. Unfortunately, he wasn't around anymore, and now that he finally knew that he needed to thank him, he couldn't.

"I guess I was just wondering where she's been staying. And wanted to let you know that if you see her, I think she's pretty harmless. Her main desire is to be with her sister."

"There's a lot of history there. From the boy that was with her to where in the world she's supposed to be and why people aren't looking for her."

"Yeah. I'll try to get to the bottom of it. But in the meantime, I'm going to try to find a place where she can stay and that might eventually adopt her sister if the option ever comes up. Kim said that her sister's foster parents were just in it for the money. I... I'm not sure I can believe that you could do a job like that just for the money, but maybe it's true." Davis lifted a hand, as though he really had no idea.

Alex concentrated on his food. It was delicious. Some kind of tater tot breakfast type casserole that was perfect after a long morning of working on the building.

Maybe he bit off more than he could chew with the construction, although... He had the confidence he could do it. It was just going to take a while. And maybe he needed that time to recharge and think. And court a certain woman he knew.

"When we're done making hay, there won't be too much to do on the farm. If you were going to do all of this yourself, if the gossip in town is true, and you're interested in any help, Luke and I would be happy to come give you a hand."

"Really?"

"Sure. Just let us know. Not that the farm doesn't keep us busy, but once the hay is in, we usually have a few weeks where things are a little bit slower."

"I can help you too. Although, I don't really know anything about what you're doing. I...didn't learn too much about building stuff in my former business."

"Yeah. If I hadn't had my uncle... I wouldn't know either." Alex studied Davis. He'd seen him around in the business world, heard about him, met him a few times, but it was going to be interesting getting to work with him. That was something he was looking forward to. Davis had a reputation of being honest.

Alex figured he could never have too many honest people around him.

By the time they were done eating, they'd completely demolished the breakfast casserole, and there was nothing left but a dirty dish.

The men took the spoons and the dish and the water jug while he took the plastic cups and paper plates and walked to the dumpster. He didn't watch the men walk away, but he had a good feeling in his chest. The feeling he had when he made a good business contact. Only that was for contacts, and he wouldn't even consider them contacts. He would consider them friends.

Chapter 19

"This is where you went to school?"

Clara looked over at Becky and nodded, smiling with one of those happy smiles that Becky was sure to be able to read saying that it was a happy time. She had almost exclusively fond memories of going to school here. She had been so sad when it had been time to leave and go to the big school down at Blueberry Beach.

"It was the best place ever. If all schools were like this, kids couldn't help but learn."

"It would be pretty cool to go to school where you can look out and see the lake and the horses every day."

"Back when we were in school, there weren't horses in the field, but the lake was there, of course. It was beautiful, and you're right. We got to enjoy it every day."

Becky didn't say anything, and Clara didn't push her. Clara suspected that perhaps Becky hadn't even gone to school last year.

But telling her that school was a wonderful thing and actually having her enjoy it herself were two different things. But she could try to give as many positive aspects to it as she could.

"I see lights on. Does that mean that the guy you said was going to be here is here?"

"Maybe. He might have left lights on after he left. Or he might still be working."

She had wanted to go see Alex all day. She managed to keep from walking up until Kim had approached her with an idea.

Apparently, they'd found out that the girl that had been working for them was homeless. She'd run away from her foster family, and they really needed to contact the authorities and deal with the issue. However, Kim had promised Becky that she would try not to let that happen. She'd come up with the idea that everyone in town would take turns housing Becky for a night, until they could discuss things with child services.

Clara had volunteered to take the first night.

Becky had come willingly and hadn't seemed afraid. She didn't exactly act belligerent, although she wasn't open or friendly either. Clara figured she had enough heartache in her life to make her suspicious of strangers.

But Clara had seen it as an opportunity to go see Alex. And using the excuse that she wanted to take Becky for a horse ride along the lake and look at the sunset, they were going to ask Alex if he wanted to come along.

It was one of the best things about living in Strawberry Sands, and Clara had wanted to do it with Alex ever since he talked about moving in. She just...couldn't really ask him to go with her by himself. Not that there was anything wrong with that exactly, she just...wasn't sure whether that would be something that he would be interested in or not. Actually, if she was being honest, she was just too scared.

"You go in the front door?" Becky asked as they reached the end of the building and needed to decide whether to walk to the front or to the back.

"Yeah. Let's go to the front."

Clara really didn't know. She was showing up here tomorrow, although she wasn't sure what she would be doing. It was doubtful that Alex had gotten anything set up. Since the truck wasn't even scheduled to arrive with their things from Chicago until tomorrow.

They heard clanging and banging as they walked around the building, and through the window, they could see Alex wearing a face mask and wielding a crowbar.

It looked like he was smacking the floor, breaking up the tile and then scraping it back.

"That looks like fun!" Becky said.

"I think there would be a certain kind of satisfaction in ripping something apart with a heavy blunt instrument," Clara said with a grin.

"Yeah. Do you think he'd let us help?"

"I'm sure he probably will. Although, if we're going to go down to get our horses saddled and ride on the beach, we better get going. Maybe we can do this tomorrow?"

She hadn't realized he was going to be working on the floor. She thought they were going to be patching things together and working out of it as they slowly hired someone to fix things up while Alex did some work on the side.

But everything was kind of new for Alex, so maybe he hadn't been sure what was going to happen. Maybe he still wasn't. He'd had some big changes in his life.

She waited until he wasn't banging on something, then knocked on the door before she opened it. It was unlocked.

At her knock on the glass, he stopped and turned.

There should be music playing, or something like that, but there wasn't. It was just Alex, dusty and dirty in a T-shirt and jeans, pulling his mask down, surprise stamped all over his face.

"Clara," he breathed.

"I'm sorry for interrupting you, Alex," she said. She liked the way her name sounded on his lips. It gave her a shiver to hear it.

"You're not interrupting anything. You know you're welcome anytime." He stared at her for just a few moments, but they seemed like an eternity, before his attention went to the little girl beside her. "You have a friend."

"Oh. Yes. This is Becky. She's staying with me tonight."

"You must be the little girl everybody was talking about at lunch today."

"Everybody?" Clara lifted her brows, looking around at the obviously empty school. "Do you have multiple personalities?" she asked, and she was mostly teasing.

"You know I don't. I can hardly handle the personality I have." They laughed a little. "Your brothers were here, along with Davis. I think you know Davis, don't you, Becky?" He wiped his hand on his pants and took three steps forward with it out to shake Becky's.

She stared at it for a moment before she touched it carefully.

"Nice to meet you, Becky," he said.

"Nice to meet you," she said a little uncertainly. "And I know Davis. I take care of his horses."

"They're beautiful. You do a good job."

"Thanks." She still didn't sound completely comfortable, and Clara wasn't sure whether that was because she was afraid Alex would figure out that she wasn't legit and try to cart her away, or whether it made her uncomfortable to know that people had been talking about her.

Whichever it was, Clara wanted to get the situation back on firm footing.

"Would you be interested in taking a horse ride with us this evening? Becky's mine for tonight, and I wanted to go horseback riding along the beach while the sun went down." She tried not to sound too enthusiastic. Sometimes, people could push things so hard that they ended up pushing people away, instead of talking them into it. But she couldn't help adding, "It's my favorite part about living in Strawberry Sands."

"Riding horses on the beach?"

"Yeah. At sunset. It's the best."

"Yeah. Horses, sunsets, beaches, and great company are the best things Strawberry Sands has to offer," he said easily, taking the mask and pulling it over his head, throwing the crowbar on the floor. "I'd say I need to clean up my mess, but the point is kind of to make one right now, so no need."

"Wow. I just thought we were going to bring the stuff in and kind of set up the way it was."

"That's what I was thinking when we were looking at it before. But I decided I wanted to make it so that you would have an office with that big window that faces out to the lake. So I'm going to need to do some rearranging."

"Wow. Really?" Her heart flipped. He was going to take care of her like that? Give her the very best spot in the entire school?

She could hardly believe it.

"It's important to me that you have a good view. If you're going to try to make a living with your paintings... I guess I haven't really figured out how you're going to do that and still work for me, but maybe we'll cross that bridge some other time."

"Let's not do it tonight," she said, agreeing with him. She didn't know how she was going to do it either. She really didn't want to not work for him anymore. And the fact that he bought the school confirmed that. She wanted to be there every day. She loved this building, loved this view, loved everything about this area. She didn't want to go somewhere else.

"No. Tonight, we're going horseback riding on the horses that Becky takes care of. Which one should I ride?" he asked, looking at Becky, who straightened a little at his praise.

Clara suspected that Becky hadn't been praised much of her life, and she appreciated the fact that Alex seemed to know instinctively that she needed it.

Then of course, she remembered Alex's background, and she bet that he could sympathize if not relate to Becky.

"Well, Winter is a good one. But he'll probably not go any faster than a walk. So if you want one that's going to go slow for you, Winter is a good one."

"I think I might want Winter," Clara said with a smile and a small laugh.

"All right. Clara gets Winter. Now, what about me?" Alex asked as he flipped the lights off after looking around to make sure everything was ready to go.

He walked to the door and held it open while Becky and Clara walked through. As Clara went through, her eyes met his for just a moment, and she saw...happiness and warmth in them. It settled down in her soul and made her feel like he was thrilled that she had come up and enjoyed spending time with her. Wanted to spend time with her.

Maybe she was just extrapolating the way she felt onto him. Because that was the way she felt, like she wanted to spend time with him.

She almost stopped in the doorway. But somehow, her feet managed to keep moving, and that little contact was broken.

"You'll want to ride Tony. He's tall, and so are you," Becky said, and Clara was happy that she seemed to be unaware of the change of tension in the air.

There was just something about being with Alex. There always had been, but it was more intense now. Whether it was because they were in Strawberry Sands, or whether it was because of the changes in his life. Or maybe, it was her thinking about quitting that had made him realize that...there could be more.

Whatever it was, it made her want to be with him as much as she could. It had been hard enough to stay away all day.

The idea of quitting now didn't sit right.

"Does he listen?" Alex asked easily. "I'm not much of a horse rider, and I don't think I'm going to want to ride a horse that's gonna run away with me."

"Oh, Mr. Davis and Miss Kim don't have any horses like that. They're all really nice. A couple of them are a little spookier than others, but I think you could ride any of them and be happy."

"All right, Tony it is. Who are you going to ride?" he asked as they started down the hill, Alex on one side of Becky and Clara on the other.

"Silver is my favorite. She's pretty. Plus, she's nice. She walks up to me in the pasture every time I go out. And when I'm cleaning her stall, she just wants to stand there and watch me. It's like she likes me."

Clara could hear that longing in her voice. The longing that everyone had for someone to like them just for them.

Maybe Alex heard it too because he said, "I think Silver has really good taste. Because I've heard that you take excellent care of the horses. In fact, Davis just told me today that he was so happy that he had someone that he could trust to take care of them while his daughter was in the NICU. I know he appreciates what you do."

Clara smiled because she could almost feel Becky growing beside her, just basking in the praise.

She wasn't sure whether there would ever be enough praise to make Becky feel like she was worth something, only God could do that, but there was just a need in every person to know that at least one other person in the world thought they were worth something.

Of course, she loved that Alex was willing to be the person who would make someone else feel worthy.

They chatted as they walked down the hill and to the stables. Clara had already talked to Davis and Kim, and when they heard that Becky was going to be with them, they said everything was fine. She got the feeling that Davis and Kim wanted to do more for Becky, but they could only do what Becky would allow.

They'd already offered their home, and Becky hadn't wanted that.

Still, they trusted her with the horses, and Clara made sure that Becky knew that when Davis and Kim had heard that she was going to be with them, they hadn't felt the need to come out.

They hadn't charged them either. It was almost like they were offering to take their daughter for a ride.

Clara had grown up on a farm, and she'd ridden horses some, but she was a little rusty because it had been a while. Still, they managed to get them tacked up, and they led them to the edge of the barn.

"Looks like we're right on time. The sun is going down, and the lake is calm." She loved how the wind seemed to settle at dawn and dusk, even for just a little bit. As she looked out on the lake, it looked like smooth glass, like she could touch it and it would be solid.

"A beautiful night for a ride," Alex said from behind her, and his comment warmed her heart. There was something in the tone of his voice that made her think that maybe he was saying a little bit more.

"There's the dog that hangs around," Becky said, peering off into the dusky light.

"It's the Great Pyrenees that runs around Strawberry Sands."

He padded closer, and his big furry body came into view.

"He's pretty," Clara said, bending down to pet him. "I heard he hangs around Kim and Davis's place a good bit."

"They feed him here."

"That explains it," Clara said. "But I thought he was hanging around more up near the schoolhouse. In fact, I was surprised we haven't seen him."

"I actually did see him today," Alex said, sounding thoughtful. "He... He just hung out with me for a little bit. He didn't seem to need attention or even want it. He just wanted to be with me."

"He's really chill," Becky said, walking forward, putting both of her hands in his hair.

Clara and Alex exchanged glances. Clara couldn't say for sure what Alex was thinking, but she was thinking that Becky needed something to love. Like a dog.

Although, the dog didn't hang out here exclusively. And he didn't follow Becky around. He seemed to be free to roam.

Regardless, she forgot about the dog as they mounted their horses and rode along the beach. He didn't follow, and he wasn't there when they got back. Clara put him out of her mind.

Chapter 20

"Are you eating more of those chocolate-covered espresso beans?" Sunday stood at the counter in the kitchen area of the bed-and-breakfast.

There weren't too many guests milling about at this hour, and it was just Lana, with a handful of espresso beans, along with Sunday and Clara, and a wide-awake Becky.

Becky had been awake since well before the sun came up, but Clara had convinced her that there was no need to get up until at least dawn started to break.

The kitchen smelled like coffee, but her mom was crunching on the beans like she'd found her new addiction. She popped another one in her mouth.

"You would not believe how good these things are," she said, and then she closed her eyes like she needed time and space to enjoy it.

Clara met Sunday's eyes, and they laughed and shook their heads.

Their mom didn't typically eat candy at all, and she wasn't big into chocolate either. It was kind of odd that she was falling in such love with the beans.

"Where did you get them to begin with?" Clara asked. Her mom never even bought candy. That she knew of anyway. "When we were kids, you never had junk food sitting around the house."

"Well, I had to keep you guys healthy. So I kept it for a treat, made it an indulgence once in a while." Lana popped another one in her mouth and chewed before she answered Clara's first question while she poured herself a cup of freshly brewed coffee. "You remember the man we saw when we took our last walk along the beach?"

"The one who lives in the lighthouse? The one that you said you worry about occasionally?"

"Yes. That one. I kinda think that his son doesn't like to visit, so he just sends stuff instead," her mom said with a little bit of a condescending tone in her voice. That surprised Clara. Typically, her mom didn't talk badly about anyone. "So his son sent them, and he gave them to me."

Her affection for the older man was obvious.

"And the man doesn't like them?"

"He didn't really say," her mom said, popping another bean into her mouth. "He just said that he thought I might like them, and he gave them to me the last time I was walking out there."

"Which was yesterday?"

"The day before. Yesterday was pretty busy, and I didn't get out."

"Well, I'm pretty sure you shouldn't eat too many of those at one time. They do have a lot of caffeine in them," Sunday said, with her brows drawn together, like she was actually worried about their mom.

"I only eat them in the morning. I think you're right. I do feel a jolt from them, but they're so good." She looked at the last one she held in her hand. "That was five. I could probably have a couple more." She put one in her mouth and walked to the bag, carefully pulling out two more and looking at Clara after she did so, as though she were checking to see if she were being watched or not. Like a kid with her hand in the cookie jar, trying to figure out whether she could get away with taking two cookies instead of just one.

"I only got two," Lana said.

Clara wanted to say she didn't care how many chocolate-covered espresso beans her mom ate, but it was interesting to see her mom go a little crazy over something so simple. She was happy to see her happy.

Of course, with that thought, she remembered the night before, riding with Alex on the beach. He made her own heart happy.

Funny how finding someone who seemed to understand a person, or seemed to really care about them, could make a person's life so much...brighter. They hadn't even really talked too much last night. The long moment that they'd spent staring into each other's eyes as she walked out of the school had been the only thing that could be considered romantic in the entire evening.

Beyond that, their attention had been on Becky, like they'd determined without saying anything that Becky would have a fantastic evening with them together. Maybe they just wanted to let her know that people cared about her. Clara wasn't sure, but she felt like Alex and she communicated without talking. She felt like that before when they were working, but it was one thing to work with someone and work well with them, it was a completely different thing to hang out with them and feel the same way.

She hoped her mom found someone like that. She deserved it after so many years alone and after what her ex had done to her. She was an amazing woman, and she deserved someone who appreciated her and loved her for who she was.

Not the lighthouse dude, who was way too old. Even if she did love his chocolate-covered espresso beans.

"You know, you guys should try these. I think you'll both love them. Especially you, Sunday, because you love coffee so much, and chocolate."

"I would try them, Mom. But I see how addicted you are to them already, and you only had them a day. The last thing I need in my life is more addictions. Or bad habits."

Clara didn't say anything, but she felt a little bad for her sister. Her life hadn't quite gone as smoothly as she had hoped it would, and she had scars from it.

She supposed along with her mom, she wished things would go well for her sister too. Maybe they would both find a lifetime love that they could share their lives with.

"Are you ready to go, kiddo?" she asked as Becky pulled a doughnut off the table and stuck it in her mouth.

"Yep," Becky said around the doughnut.

"Don't talk with your mouth full, sweetie," Lana said, and Clara appreciated that. She hadn't been sure whether she should correct the child or not. She hated to, since the kid wasn't hers, but at the same time, since she didn't exactly have a mom and dad to guide her as she grew, maybe she needed that kind of discipline from whoever was in her life.

Regardless, her mother took care of it in her lovingly casual way. Becky nodded and obediently kept her mouth closed until after she swallowed.

"I know I shouldn't, but I just forgot."

"That's okay. Nobody's perfect, and I know what I should do all the time too, but sometimes I forget, and sometimes I can't get myself to do the right thing. We just have to keep trying."

She nodded, and Clara figured that was probably about the best thing that her mom could say. After all, who didn't like to know that other people made mistakes too?

She opened the door, and Becky went out in front of her. She wasn't exactly the carefree little girl that Clara wished she could be, but it did seem like she felt like there were people who cared about her now, where before she had been a little more withdrawn and secretive. Maybe it was because she was afraid of being found out.

"Kristin gets you next." She started the conversation as they walked down the driveway and sidewalk, turning toward Kristin's house where she lived with her gram and her gram's two friends. It was almost a private assisted living center, with all of the older ladies that lived there.

She had a feeling that it might be a little bit boring for Becky. Although Kristin was super sweet, and Kristin could probably use a bit of a distraction from her gram constantly trying to match her up.

"I like Alex. You and he make a nice couple," Becky said as they walked across the street.

"We're not really a couple. He's just my boss. And we're going to be working together here in Strawberry Sands now." She wished they were a couple. And she liked hearing Becky say they made a good one. But even though she hoped that was the direction the relationship was taking, she wasn't quite sure, and she didn't want to give any illusions that it was more than what it was. First of all, she didn't want to upset Alex, and second, she didn't want to get her own hopes up.

Which was harder and harder to do. She loved the idea that maybe her dreams were coming true.

"You weren't acting like a couple last night."

"No. We were going riding with you."

"Why did you ask him to go with us?"

"Well, he's a city boy, I guess. And he's my boss, so I did hope he would agree to go for a ride. I think he enjoyed it. He's the kind of person who has a tendency to work too hard."

"I guess that's probably true, especially since he was working way after everyone else had already quit for the day."

"When you're old enough to be looking for a guy, you do want to find one who works hard. You don't want to be married to someone who would rather play than work or complains about working. Can you imagine being married to someone who complains about his job for the rest of your life?" She couldn't imagine that.

"I guess it's no fun when someone else complains, although it always feels good to complain yourself."

"Pretty wise statement for a young kid. It took me a long time to figure that out."

"People say I'm smart for my age."

Clara figured that was because she'd had to grow up faster than a kid should, but Becky seemed to have a level head on her shoulders, and if they were able to get her into a home that would love her and help her, maybe she'd be given what she needed in order to grow into a healthy adult.

"I know people have been talking about homes for you, and I just want you to know that if you want to stay with me, I'd be happy to have you—I'd love it, in fact."

Becky smiled and nodded, but she continued down the stone sidewalk and didn't say anything. It left Clara with the idea that either she was still thinking about it, or she had someone else in mind.

"Clara!" The sound of Miss Heather's voice jerked Clara out of her thoughts.

She looked over to see Miss Heather, Kristin's gram, standing on the porch of Kristin's house.

"And that must be Becky. We've been waiting on you for the last hour and a half. You need to come in here right away. We are going to make cookies today. Although, first, we're going to go get your little sister. I've decided I'm going to march right up that street, and I'm going to insist that she get to come down here and spend the day with you!"

Miss Heather's hands were on her hips, although Becky figured that if the old lady was going to march anywhere, it would have been fifty years ago. She didn't look capable of any type of marching whatsoever, unless she did it with her walker.

Which didn't make her threat any less true.

And from the way Becky had perked up at the idea of seeing her sister, Clara figured that was the best thing that could happen to her today.

Kristen came out on the porch, followed by the two ladies that lived with them.

"I think you're going to have a good day," Clara said, putting her arm around Becky. Becky didn't hesitate but leaned into her.

"Thanks for letting me stay with you," Becky said, looking up at Clara. "I want to stay in Strawberry Sands. I want to be near my sister. I guess I don't even care who I live with, as long as I'm close to her."

Clara nodded. "I think the whole town is behind you. And we're working to do everything we can to make sure that you and your sister aren't separated. And if we can get you in the same household, that would be even better."

Her words made Becky smile, which made Clara's heart happy. She knew she would do everything she could, even upending her life by adopting a child, or two children, if that's what was necessary. Although, she had a feeling she was going to have to fight the rest of the residents, because everyone seemed to have fallen in love with Becky. And they seemed to have gotten on board with her desire to be with her sister. It was something that pretty much everyone could understand.

"She's not kidding. You're gonna have a great day," Clara said to Becky as Kristin came down the steps to greet them.

"We've been looking forward to it. In case you haven't noticed, my grandma's pretty excited." Kristin smiled at Becky and walked right up to her, putting her arms around her and giving her a hug.

She stepped back a little and said in a softer voice only Becky and Clara could hear, "And if you could convince her to stop chasing men away from me by trying to grab every man in sight and shove him in my face, that would be super helpful as well. I'd like to get married sometime in the next decade."

Kristin rolled her eyes while Becky laughed, enjoying the idea that she was involved in a conspiracy.

Clara laughed, but she still felt bad for Kristin. Her grandma seemed to be the surest way that anyone had ever had of staying single for eternity.

"I'll be working today, but if you need me, my boss is a pretty great person, and I can probably come anytime."

"My grandma has her eye on your boss," Kristin said with an eye roll.

Clara wanted to immediately say her boss was not available, but actually, Alex and Kristin would make a great couple. Especially with all the changes that Alex was making.

However, after their long chat in his office, she was feeling like...maybe he really would be taken. By her.

"All right. You guys have a great day," Clara said as she gave Becky another hug, which Becky returned, waved to the ladies on the porch, and continued walking down the street. She'd walk along the beach and go up the hill until she got to the school. It was a walk she'd taken all the time when she was a kid on her way to school. Up until she had to get on the big yellow bus and be driven to Blueberry Beach for high school.

She always looked forward to going to school, and she had to admit, today she was looking forward to work. And not just because she loved her job. Actually, she didn't even know what she was going to be doing today. Possibly demolition work.

The thing she was looking forward to was seeing Alex.

Her phone buzzed, and she pulled it out of her pocket, looking at the sky and the lake and breathing deep, so grateful to be alive and have such a beautiful place to live...and work. It hadn't sunk in that her job was actually not in Chicago anymore—she worked in the best town in the world, the one she grew up in, Strawberry Sands.

Her heart stumbled as she read the text from Alex.

> **I have some personal issues in Chicago and need to leave right away. All there is to do here is demolition work. You can have another day off. You deserve it.**

She stared at her phone. Really? He was just going to leave for "personal issues?" In all the years they'd worked together, she couldn't remember him taking any time off for personal issues. Except that once with his gram and getting her into a nursing home.

Without thinking about it too much, she sent a text back.

> **I'll help you.**

That seemed rather bold, and she held her breath waiting for him to respond. After a full minute of waiting, she had almost given up that he would and had started to shove her phone back in her pocket, taking a couple of slow steps toward the school, when it buzzed.

> **Okay. I'll wait until you get here.**

> **Be there in three.**

She couldn't keep herself from smiling. He was going to allow her to help him with whatever personal issues he was having. It felt like a gift or another breakthrough in their relationship. Instinctively she knew that whatever they got into today, it would strengthen the bond between them, and while that scared her a little, she also looked forward to it.

Chapter 21

Clara had offered to come along.

Alex stared at his phone, still hardly able to believe it. She was going with him.

That thought sent a thrill through his entire body. The fact that she would even offer. Of course, he was paying her, and maybe she felt guilty for taking another day off. She had one of the best work ethics of anyone he knew.

But he wanted it to be more. He wanted her to want to go with him, not because of work, but because she liked him.

He supposed that was why it was so dangerous to be involved with someone he worked with. Especially when he was her boss. He didn't know whether she was doing what she was doing because she liked him, or because she felt responsible.

He put away the tools he had gotten out, thankful that he hadn't gotten too dirty yet that morning, and walked to the door where he saw her coming up over the hill and heading over the parking lot.

He walked out.

"If you're doing this just because you think you need to because I'm paying you, you don't have to go. It's a personal thing."

"Good morning to you, too," she said cheerfully. Then she added simply, "I want to."

Clara was one of the most upright people he knew. Sincere, and whatever she said, she truly meant. She didn't just say things.

He loved that about her.

So she said that she wanted to go.

That was all he needed to hear.

"What's the problem?" she asked as she came closer, concern etched over her face, and he felt like whatever he needed her to do, she was ready to pitch in.

He loved having someone like that in his corner. And not for the first time, but maybe for the first time consciously, he wondered what it would be like to be with her for the rest of his life. To have someone like that who would support him and help him whatever came along, just because that was the kind of person she was. What would it be like to be married to her?

He really didn't have to ask himself the question. Whoever ended up marrying Clara was getting an amazing woman.

Was it selfish for him to hope that it would be him?

"It's my gram," he said as she met him and they walked toward his car. "The nursing home that she's in—I put her in it a few years ago. You were here." He said here, meaning that she was working for him at the time.

"I remember."

Funny that she would remember. Of course, he didn't remember talking about it much at work at all. He had always been a big believer in keeping his personal life personal and out of his work life, but Clara was so easy to talk to. He had let a few things slip to her that he never had with anyone before.

"Apparently the workers have gone on strike. The administrative staff called me and asked if it was at all possible, I should try to get my gram moved somewhere else. They're not able to get enough temporary workers to keep up the quality of care."

"If I recall correctly, your grandma was in her right mind, she just needed help with everyday living."

"That's correct." He almost took her into his house. If he didn't have to travel so much for his business, he would have. But he thought his gram would be better off in an assisted care facility where she would have people to interact with every day, rather than spending twelve or fourteen or more hours alone every day while he worked.

Maybe it wasn't the best decision, but he'd done the best he could at the time.

"Is she still like that?" Clara asked as he opened her door. Maybe that was too gallant of a gesture for their relationship and the level they were at, but he... He wanted to open it for her. Not that she couldn't, it was just something nice he could do, something to show that he respected and cared for her.

She smiled and murmured thank you, and it made him feel like maybe he'd done the right thing.

Walking around the car, he got in, strangely looking forward to the drive to Chicago now that Clara was beside him.

"She's still completely in her right mind. Sharp as a tack. Her physical ability is slowly declining, but she works hard to stay in shape. It's kind of impressive to me."

"It doesn't really surprise me. If she's your grandmother."

He wasn't sure what that meant, but he thought it was a compliment. "Thank you, I think."

He started pulling out as she smiled at him. "It was a compliment. You are one of the most determined people I know. Hardworking, but not so driven that you will ride over anyone in your way. I've always admired that about you. That you hold to your integrity. I guess I just kind of thought that those qualities, your determination to move forward, and your drive to succeed possibly were inherited from your grandmother."

"I hadn't thought of that, but I suppose you could be right. We led very different lives, but she was successful in her own right, and she hasn't gone into old age quietly or without fighting it. She's definitely one of the people I admire most in the world." He hadn't thought about that in years, but it was true. He did admire his gram. She hadn't had an easy life, but she made the best of everything she had, and even in her 90s, she worked to stay fit and mentally sharp. Unfortunately, she had been living in Nevada while he'd been growing up, and she hadn't known about his situation. He was sure she would have helped if she could.

"In fact, I'm eager for you to meet her. Thank you for offering to come. This...isn't exactly in your job description."

"I kind of feel like maybe I'll be getting a new job description. You're shuffling things around, and...maybe my position will be eliminated?" she said with a little bit of humor in her voice, and he remembered that she really probably wasn't worried about losing her job. She had something she wanted to do anyway.

"You would be the last person I would eliminate. But I've been doing a lot of thinking."

"Okay?"

"Maybe I'm not doing the best thing for you by insisting that you stay with me. Maybe..." He didn't say love, but he felt that sometimes love meant letting go. He would let her go to do the things that she felt was best. That she felt God had for her. If he held her back, if he kept her close to himself, that didn't exactly show love. It showed that he was being selfish. Right?

"Maybe what?" she asked, looking at the horses grazing in the pasture as they drove by.

"Maybe if I truly want the best for you, I'll insist that you start your own business and try to make a living from your art."

She was silent, contemplative, maybe, as she stared at the horses, beautiful against the blue of the lake and the green grass. The early morning sun made their shadows long as dew on the grass sparkled.

"I don't know that I want to try to make my art something that I make a living on. I guess I wouldn't mind having a shop and selling it in the summer, maybe even just open it for a few hours in the afternoon and evening when things get busy. Like from one to seven or something. But... I seem to be mentioning your integrity and your character quite a lot, but it's the truth. Working for you... I feel like I'm doing good in the world. Because I'm helping one of the good guys get better. Do better. Be better. You are making a difference in the world, maybe not for your business, but through the people you touch and the way you act and the money that you've made without stealing or double-crossing people but by holding to the values that Christians hold to. It's not exactly something that happens a lot in today's world. I don't even know that people notice, because so many people assume that if you're successful, you somehow have been crooked in getting there."

She'd mentioned more than once about admiring him, and it never failed to make his chest swell. More than anyone else in the world, he cared about Clara's opinion of him. And she saw him more intimately than almost anyone else. In fact, he couldn't think of anyone who knew him and his business better than she did.

The fact that she still admired him shocked him a little but gave him hope as well.

"What are you going to do with your gram?" she asked, changing the subject, maybe misinterpreting his silence. Maybe she didn't want to talk about that and she'd searched for something else to say.

He certainly didn't mind talking about how much she admired him, but he went with the subject change, because they needed to talk about it.

"I thought I'd bring her back home with me. The last time I tried to get her into a nursing home, the waiting list for some of them was months or even years long. I don't think I'm going to be able to switch her that quickly. Hiring personal care aides, as a Band-Aid, might be difficult with the tight labor market. Plus, I'm not in Chicago anymore, I'm in Strawberry Sands. So... I'm going to bring her home."

"I think she'll like that."

"You know anyone that I could hire on a part-time basis to help me take care of her?"

"I'll think about it," she said easily, and he knew she would. A lot of times, he had asked her questions like that in his business, and she'd come through for him, coming up with the best solution, sometimes an even better solution than something he thought.

"With me needing to take care of my gram and having her live with me... I had wanted to do the work inside myself, but I was thinking that I was going to make a few phone calls and see if I couldn't get it done, today." He laughed a little. "I might not be able to get the school finished today, but I know I can get people in there that will make short work of it. I just don't know if I can get them in immediately. A lot of times, contractors have a waiting list."

"I know my brothers will help. I can make a phone call, and they might not be quite as fast or professionally streamlined as the contractors you would get, but I know it will get done, and they'll do a good job."

"We couldn't ask them. That would put them out."

"They're my brothers. That's what family is for." She sounded incredulous, like she couldn't even believe he would suggest such a thing.

Then he realized. That was the difference between his life and hers. The big city and the small town. People looked out for each other.

Even as he was thinking that, she said, "Actually, I bet the whole town will show up. Maybe they will get it done today. I'll make a call?"

"I have the specs. And I'll pay."

"So, I'll make the call. Matt will probably be the point person since he's the oldest, and you'll just tell him what you want. And I'll give him my credit card number, and you can reimburse me."

"I can give him my credit card number." He didn't usually hand it out like candy, but if Clara trusted her brother with hers, surely he could trust him with his.

They're not your family.

He had a feeling that didn't matter, and he tried to shut the voice in his head up. He wasn't used to people being kind, or considerate, or loving him.

Was that what this was? Christians loving each other?

He was always a big believer in action, not words. He had a few relationships with women who spouted out the words after just one evening together. An evening of dinner and entertainment. A function, possibly one where he even hired her. They said the words so easily, but there was no action backing them up.

He liked the action kind of love. The one where he could see that people actually meant what they said because their action said it.

She hadn't waited for him to say anything more. She was already talking to her brother. He assumed it was Matt, although if she said his name, he hadn't heard it.

"Of course. Get Luke and Ryan involved. Ryan especially because he's got more experience than either one of you two."

"Oh, he does? I hadn't realized."

She glanced over at him with a happy smile on her face. He had no idea what she was smiling about, but he returned it, then looked back at the road, making sure he got on the right interchange as he turned toward the on-ramp to head south for Chicago.

The ride was going faster than it ever had, but he supposed that was what happened when a person was in good company.

It wasn't much longer when she got off the phone, a triumphant look on her face. "They're good to go. I already explained that you're doing demolition work. But if you want to send them specific instructions, I can drive."

His first inclination was to decline her offer. But why not? Typically when he was in the car, he was the driver. He liked to have that control. But part of the reason he liked the control was so he could protect himself from other people. He liked to play by the rules and have ethics and values and character in his work, but he never assumed that someone else was going to go into a relationship with him in the same way.

Except, he knew Clara would.

Putting his turn signal on, he pulled off on the side of the road.

He had to smile at her surprised look. She was not expecting him to take her up on her offer.

"It's because I trust you." He didn't have to ask why she was surprised, and she knew exactly what he was saying because her lips turned up and she nodded a happy nod.

He got out, a truck whishing by, almost knocking him down.

It made him want to take a hold of Clara as she came around the front of the car.

"The wind from the semi is more fierce than what you think," he said, like that gave him an excuse to put his arm around her to guide her to his door.

She curved into his side and seemed to fit there just perfectly.

He didn't typically walk around with his arm around her, in fact never had, and while it was a new feeling, he couldn't deny it was a perfect one.

Another semi went by, and the air from that pushed against them.

"My goodness. You don't realize there's that much power when you're driving beside them."

He opened the door, and she hopped in.

Maybe they shouldn't have stopped along the road, but it seemed like it would be smarter to stop and switch places than for him to try to do the business from his phone.

Regardless, she was safely inside, and soon they were on the road again.

"Did you even call your grandma and let her know you are coming?" she asked as she got up to road speed and set the cruise.

"Actually...I haven't."

"Maybe she'll want to pack."

Chapter 22

"Do you think I should remove my gram permanently?" Alex hadn't even been thinking in that direction. He figured he'd just take her until the facility could take her again. Until they got the strike or whatever it was worked out. But... She could pack up and move to Strawberry Sands.

Before, when he put her in the assisted care facility, he'd done it because he didn't want her home for hours on end without him. But with him working in Strawberry Sands and with Clara being there... Of course, she hadn't said for sure that she was staying, but she did encourage him with the thought that maybe she wasn't completely thinking about quitting. They hadn't pursued that line of conversation, and maybe it was a deliberate thing on his part, since he didn't want to hear that she couldn't.

Maybe he should have. Because he was curious now.

"I think that's up to you. And her too. Maybe she won't want to leave."

"If I know my grandma, even a little, she will be thrilled at the opportunity to live in Strawberry Sands. And I would be willing to bet she would love living in the old schoolhouse. She used to be a teacher."

"She was?"

"A long time ago, before she was married, she taught school in a one-room schoolhouse. I probably wouldn't know it, but she talked fondly about that time in her life. I think if she had been born in a different time period, she probably would have been a teacher all her life, but when she got married, she quit."

"I hope she loves what she did with the rest of her life."

"She did. I don't really think she regretted it, she just looked back on it with fondness. She loved being a wife and a mother. And from what I understand, she was a good one."

"I love that. People who have a path in life, and they walk that path determined to enjoy every second of it. It seems like a waste of life to be miserable, you know?"

Boy, did he ever. "If there's anything that you taught me, that's probably it. Although, that was such an understatement. I learned a lot from you. But being content where I'm at is probably one of the biggest."

"I suppose it's easier to be content where you're at when you're sure that God has you exactly where you are. And is using you for His purpose. After all, if you're sure about that, then where you are and what you're doing is the exact right thing, so why would you be unhappy about it?"

"If you take that out even further, the things other people do won't bother you, because you have your eyes fixed on Jesus."

"Exactly. But I think that's where we stumble as humans. Because we want to be offended. We want to get upset. We want to have our rights and our way. In our society, we're taught that we can't allow people to take advantage of us. That there's something wrong with us if we allow people to take advantage."

"Classic blame the victim, but it's an acceptable teaching all through society."

"I don't want to be considered a victim of them. I'm not. Being a victim insinuates that you can't help where you are. You can't be a victim if you've chosen to allow someone else to do things that take away from your supposed rights."

He nodded. "You know, I've always enjoyed discussing things like this with you."

"We haven't done it very often," she said, laughing a little, like she found what he had intended as a compliment to be amusing instead.

"No. I guess we always did keep things work related. That's just...the way I do it, I guess."

"Well, that's the thing I admire about you. You are always very professional. I never wondered if there was something going on between you and anyone else that you were working with, because while you were kind, you worked with some women who flocked after you, thinking that you thought more of them than what you did. There is always a very solid line between work and personal. And you don't allow anyone to cross it."

"You have." He heard the deeper note in his voice, and he figured that was just his emotions coming out. Because it was true. What she said was accurate, because he'd always been very careful to be professional and moral. He didn't want there to be any office gossip about him and anyone else. And he certainly didn't want anything along those lines to be true. Except with Clara.

"It took seven years," she said. Her tone was light, but he felt like there was a deeper message to what she said.

"Maybe that's because I didn't think that you liked me. At all."

"Why else would I have stayed with you for seven years?"

Was that true?

"Was I so terrible to work with for that long?"

She shook her head no but didn't comment.

"I'm confused."

"About what?" she asked, as though they hadn't just been talking about personal versus business, and she made a comment that made him feel like maybe she had feelings for him. Was she really not going to explain it?

"Why did you work for me for seven years?"

She was quiet for a while, and he appreciated that. He felt like she was taking his question seriously and she would give him an accurate answer. Because after all, she'd already said that she admired his integrity and his character. But that wasn't what kept her at her job.

"Was it the money?" he finally asked. Maybe he had totally misunderstood, and she was making a comment about the salary he paid her. It was higher than any other administrative assistant he knew. He believed in compensating a person for doing a good job, and he couldn't imagine that there was anyone else in the world, and he'd been around a good bit, who could do what Clara did, who could know him so well, understand him, and work to please him.

"No."

"I didn't think so. Why?" he pushed. Because he really wanted to know. He felt like he was on the cusp of finding out something that was going to change his life. And that seemed like an overstatement, but it wasn't. He was pretty sure that Clara's answer to that question was going to point him down a different path.

"You're going to laugh at me," she finally said.

"I promise I won't."

"I'm going to be embarrassed."

"If I can fix that, I will."

"I had a crush on you."

"For seven years?" He didn't mean to question her, he just couldn't believe it. He had no idea. "You have to know you shocked me."

"Seriously? You didn't know?" She turned her head and looked at him, as though truly unsure as to whether or not he might have known.

"No."

"Would it have changed anything?"

He wanted to shout "yes" into the car interior, but he didn't want to say something without thinking it through. But... Of course it would have changed everything. He would have... He didn't even know.

"Yes. I'm sure it would have changed things. I'm not sure how. But it changes them now."

"How so?" she asked, and she sounded a little fatalistic, like she was resigned to whatever he was going to say but knew she wasn't going to like it.

"You don't like the fact that you had a crush on me?" And then he realized he said it in the past tense. "Do you still? Have a crush, I mean?"

"I don't know if you can call it a crush. A crush kind of sounds temporary. Seven years isn't really temporary, is it?"

"Seven years is a good long time. Maybe longer than what you should have allowed it to go on. Why didn't you ever say anything?"

"Have you ever seen the girls you go out with?" she asked, and there was a hint of humor in her eyes.

"I guess." He stared at them for an entire night. He'd seen them. But it was usually someone he had hired which saved him the trouble of maintaining a relationship and kept him from having to go places alone. That seemed to invoke more speculation than the parade of different women that he'd been with over the years. "Only for one night."

"I'm not exactly like them."

"No. I guess you're not."

She gave an easy smile. "You know. I'm a small-town girl, living in Strawberry Sands. You... You hire people to go out with you, and they want to. Some of them, you didn't even have to pay. Just for the prestige of being on your arm."

"That's true." He sounded a little sad about that, probably because he was. He hadn't realized how that might look to her. Hadn't really given it a thought. It was just a means to an end. He needed to go, needed to go with someone, and he had Clara hire someone for him.

"It had never occurred to me that you would go with me."

"I don't know that I would have."

"Your question involves being seen in public with me?"

"My question involves being out in public... Not necessarily with you, but...at an event for you. I... I didn't want to be just your business call girl."

"None of them were ever call girls." He wanted to be clear about that.

"I didn't mean it that way. I think you know what I meant."

"I did. I just didn't want you to insinuate more than what happened with anyone else."

"I'm sorry. I didn't mean to."

"You don't need to apologize. I just wanted to make sure we understood each other."

"I understand." She glanced over before looking back at the road, the traffic getting heavier. "I understand. I don't belong in that world. I'm not comfortable there, and... I don't want to be there."

"So you're content with a crush, and the idea of it, but not turning it into anything that resembled reality?"

She took a breath, breathing in deeply, blowing it out. "We seem like an odd couple, don't we?"

He didn't like that. But it was true. "Maybe I'll become a small-town guy, and then we won't be so odd together."

"You know, one of the hallmarks of a bad relationship is if someone asks you to change. And I guess I agree with that in some ways. I don't think that anyone should change to make someone love them. That seems like bribery. But our love for Jesus changes us. Just as his love for us does. I'm not entirely sure that changing in a relationship, or for a relationship, is bad. It's just when someone threatens you and holds their love over your head."

"So you're telling me I'm allowed to change into a small-town boy?"

She laughed a little. "I guess I was just trying to justify that in my head. Because when someone says 'I'll change for you,' it automatically sounds wrong. Just because of the way we've been conditioned in society. But isn't that what we do for Jesus? We change for him. And isn't the relationship between a man and woman supposed to mirror the relationship between Christ and the church? So, maybe there are things that change a couple, not because of the threat of love being withheld, but because the other person is just that good for them. Or they want to do it to be a better person, someone that the person they love deserves."

He understood what she was saying, understood that it was such a far cry from what modern man considered normal, he would have to think about it for a while. He had been joking, a little bit anyway, about becoming a small-town boy for her. He didn't think he had to change in order to win her love. If that's what he was even doing. Yet he hadn't articulated that to himself at all. But sometimes changing for someone was a good thing.

"My grandma loved her husband. And she willingly gave up her teaching job, knowing she had to when she got married. That's a change, a change I love. I think today we look back on that and shake our heads and say that she sacrificed too much, but sometimes love is sacrifice."

"That's exactly right. Exactly what I was thinking. Sometimes love is sacrifice. Sometimes love is change. Sometimes love means giving up."

"Sometimes love means letting go."

She tilted her head, then slanted her eyes at him. "That's true."

"I was thinking about that. About you. About what you want with your job, and how you want your paintings, and how I was doing everything I could to get you to not leave. I just want you to know that I'll support you whatever you do. If you want a patron to back you as you step out, trying to sell your paintings and make a living from them, you can count me in."

He didn't say that to make her smile. He said it because he was sincere, but a grin split across her face.

"Really?" she asked, sounding like she couldn't believe it.

"Really."

"All right. Will you give me some time to think about it?" she asked, although it didn't really sound like a question. It sounded like she knew he was going to let her think as long as she wanted to about it.

"Of course. You just let me know when you're ready. I... I'll never be able to find someone to replace you, but I won't probably need another administrative assistant."

"Really?"

"I'm going to be downsizing, and I probably won't need as much help. I am going to stop traveling. That's for sure. I... I think it's gonna be hard for me to shut off the part of me that always wants to do more and bigger and better, but there's definitely a peaceful tranquility of living in Strawberry Sands, and I want to settle there. Permanently."

"Permanently?" She seemed like she hadn't believed that he was actually going to make the move. Hadn't he been clear?

"Yeah. I told you I spent my time in the Cities last week undoing everything I had done. Getting out of some other things and starting to wind down the business in Chicago. I'm serious. Strawberry Sands will be my home, and things are going to look a lot different."

She nodded, but they'd gotten to the point where traffic forced her to keep her attention on the road, and so he backed off.

Getting instructions for the nursing home, he connected it to his car speaker, and they drove the rest of the way in silence.

Chapter 23

Clara found a place to park in the parking area of the assisted living center. It had been an interesting drive, and she was a little bit sad that it was over. Although things between them didn't really get settled, they did seem to move forward slowly.

Alex got out, and she thought that maybe he was coming around to open her door, but she wasn't going to just sit there waiting, so she took her belt off and got out and met him at the front corner of the car.

"I know we're here for my grandma, and I feel like I need to focus on that, but... I can't stop thinking about you. I, well, you've worked with me long enough to know that when I have something I'm thinking about, I don't usually stop until I figure out a solution. I guess I'm just not sure where we stand. And...that's my fault." His tone had gotten a little uncertain, but by the time he said the last phrase, his confidence was back. "I like you. I like you a lot. And over the last few months, but especially over the last week or so. I think it's been percolating for years. I don't want anyone else to be working with me. I just want you. And I realize that... I want more. I want us to be more. I like you for more than just a secretary to see at work and then go home and not think about until the next day. I... I wondered if you might feel the same about me?"

His words made her heart flip, and even though his last question sounded a little insecure, surely he could look at her face and tell that it didn't have to be.

"I do. I definitely do." She kind of thought that that was what they had been talking about the last couple times they talked, but she hadn't come right out and said it. "I admire you, and I definitely have feelings that go beyond friendship. But you're my boss. So I have to be careful."

"You're my employee, so I have to be careful. But we can do this, right?"

She nodded. "I want to. And I have confidence that you can, because I've seen you make so many things that I thought were impossible happen, and I know that this will be a piece of cake for you."

"I'm not exactly skilled in the area of relationships. In fact, it's probably my weakest area."

"We'll do it together. We're a great team, remember?"

"That means more than what you say. I... I think that all successful people have people who believe in them standing behind them, being air for them, so to speak."

"I'm happy to be air. Especially for someone who deserves so much to have wind."

"So... If I walk in there and I'm holding your hand, you know my grandmother is going to ask us about things."

"Is that okay with you?" she asked, but she didn't look at him; instead, her eyes had dropped to his hands. She wasn't afraid. And she didn't think he was either. In fact, she thought the look in his eye was more eager than anything.

But she didn't dwell on that; instead, she moved her hand forward and touched it to his.

That was all it took before he turned and their fingers slid together, like they'd been doing it for years.

But they hadn't, and she closed her eyes for just a moment, getting used to the odd sensation of holding her boss's hand. Holding Alex's hand.

"Is that okay?" he asked. He hadn't moved. He'd given her the time she needed. Maybe it was from all the years of working together that he knew that she just needed a moment to process.

"I love it," she said, her head still down, her eyes closed.

But she opened her eyes and lifted her head, looking into his face and smiling. "It feels exactly right."

"For me too. I... Thank you." He stumbled a little like he wasn't sure what he was going to say. She wondered what he had in mind to begin with.

"My pleasure."

That made his eyes sparkle, and they turned together, walking into the assisted living center, where chaos seemed to reign. There were suitcases and bags and boxes stacked in the halls, with harried-looking residents and even more hassled-looking family members.

Clara saw one lady with a name badge on, who she assumed was an employee, but those were few and far between.

"Well. It's worse than I thought," Alex murmured as he led her down the hall, where they took a right, then a left and went down another long hall.

The people thinned out a little, but there were still bags and boxes, and it looked like the entire assisted living center was finding a new place to live.

"This is her room," Alex said as he knocked on the door. It was closed but wasn't latched. When he knocked, it opened further.

Clara noted the name on the door was Daisy Hendrix.

Daisy. That was a happy name.

Alex pushed the door open. "Gram?" he said as it swung wide.

"Alex." An older lady with straight snow white hair, parted on the side in a no-nonsense pixie cut, looked up. Her voice sounded cultured, although old. "You're here. You could have given me a little bit more notice. Normally I would be standing here telling everyone where to put everything, but it seems like all of my minions have left me, and I've had to do it for myself. It's a wonder I didn't have to cook my own breakfast this morning."

The lady straightened, and her eyes landed on Clara, who was trying to bite back a laugh.

"You're holding hands with a woman. I don't think I've seen that in your entire life. This must be special." She put a little emphasis on the word "special," a little twist that made it sound like she cared deeply about Alex. That, more than anything else, made Clara love her instantly.

"It is special. Clara, this is my grandma, Daisy. Gram, this is the special woman in my life, Clara."

"This is your administrative assistant? Your secretary? The lady you've told me about often when you visit."

"Yeah. That's Clara."

Clara could almost say that Alex's cheeks had reddened. She wasn't sure, with his stubble hiding a good portion of his cheeks, but she almost thought he was embarrassed.

Allowing her hand to slip out of Alex's hand, she put her arms out and hugged the older lady.

Daisy was not expecting it, but it didn't take long for her arms to close around and for her to squeeze. For an older lady, she gave good hugs.

She smelled like lavender and disinfectant and intelligence and cheerfulness.

"Clara. It's so nice to finally meet you. When my grandson would talk about you, I could see the look in his eye, and I would wonder if I would ever get to meet you before I passed on. I thought if there was ever going to be someone that my grandson would settle down with, it would be you."

"We haven't settled down yet."

"But we have bought a school together."

"Together?" Clara turned around and looked at him, her head tilted. She didn't really have much to do with it.

"We went to see it together? We looked at it together. We decided that we'd rather have the school than the house."

"You bought a school?" Daisy said, her wrinkled face housing shrewd green eyes that shifted between the two of them. "You probably don't need to agree on whether or not you bought it together, as long as you agree that you bought it. A school."

"Yeah. It was the school where I went to elementary school. I... I guess I must have talked rather fondly about it, and Alex is a bit of a sucker for a good story."

"I don't think anyone has ever called me a sucker, at least not for twenty years or more."

"But being a sucker for a good story is a good thing," Clara said.

He grinned at her, and they shared a smile over the space that separated them.

Then, Alex seemed to realize that he could walk closer, and he did, coming toward her and putting his arm around her as she backed away from Daisy.

"You're smiling at her. Joking even. I think this could end up being a good thing," Daisy said, tapping her finger on her chin.

"It kind of feels like we have an evacuation going on in here. Do we need to hurry and get out?" Clara said, uncomfortable under the scrutiny. She felt like Daisy was taking her measure, and she wasn't sure she would measure up. There was a part of her that felt like maybe she wasn't good enough for a man like Alex. She knew that was silly to think that. There was no human who was better or worse than another human, and she would be just as good for him as anyone else. Except a little voice told her that maybe she would be better. Because she would work to help him achieve everything he wanted to.

He knew that already. And she proved it over and over again. But wasn't it a blessing to be married to someone who only had your best interest at heart? To be married to someone who wanted to lift you up and help you be a better person?

Chapter 24

Alex walked along the beach, holding Clara's hand. He couldn't believe how things had worked out.

"Your gram was just totally in her element with Kristen and her gram and their friends." Clara seemed like she still couldn't believe how his gram had fit in with the ladies.

Really, he was surprised, too.

After they'd gotten home and the guys had still been working on the school, which was almost finished, but they had run out of supplies. Alex hadn't wanted his gram to stay in an unfinished room, so he was going to book a hotel.

"I'm so grateful you came up with the idea of paying Kristen for Gram to stay there."

"I'm happy you went along with it," Clara said, squeezing his hand as the lake breeze blew gently over them. They were just strolling, listening to the breaking waves and enjoying each other's company. "I think it's a win-win for everyone. Your mind is at ease because your gram is safe, Kristen is making money, and all the ladies have a new friend."

"I'm not sure Gram will ever want to go back to Chicago."

"Once you come to Strawberry Sands, it's pretty normal to not want to leave."

He laughed. "And here I thought that was just you and the pull you have over me."

"I have a pull?"

He tugged on her hand, and they stopped walking, turning to face each other. "A big one. Can't you see that?"

"I guess I don't. All I see is how much I like and admire you."

"Do you think that could ever be more?"

"More?"

"You could more than 'like' me?"

She paused while his heart hammered in his chest.

"I think I already do."

He allowed the breath he had been holding to blow out slowly. "That's good to hear because I love you. I have for a while, but the move and all the things that have happened have made me see what I couldn't before. I'd rather give up everything in my company than lose you."

He stepped closer and put a hand on her waist. She didn't move away.

"Do you think there's a future for us?"

"Aren't you going to allow me to tell you that I love you?"

His laugh was nervous. "I wasn't sure you did. I...didn't want to hear you say you needed to think about it."

"I love you. I've had a crush on you forever, but it would be impossible to know where you came from, what you've done and see the integrity and character with which you've done it and not fall in love with you." She put her hand on his chest, then slid it up to his shoulder, stepping closer. "So, yes. I see a future for us. I'm not sure what that looks like, because I don't want you giving up everything for me, but I definitely see us together. We can work something out, can't we?"

"I know I can. Anything is on the table to be cut in order for me to be with you. You're that important to me."

"And I don't want any of those things to be cut unless it's something that you want to let go."

"Maybe if we have kids I can be a stay at home dad while you create art during the day and hang out with us at night."

"Kids?" she squeaked out, and he realized that maybe he should kiss her first before he started talking about things like kids and forever.

"Kiss?" he said.

"Kiss and kids?"

"Kiss first. Kids...we'll talk about that."

She smiled and lifted her head while his lowered and he kissed her while the waves rolled and the breeze blew and the horses on the hill ate like his world hadn't just shifted in the very best way possible. Clara was going to be with him and they were going to plan a future together. It hardly seemed possible, but he stopped trying to figure that out and just enjoyed kissing her instead.

Epilogue

Kristen flipped an egg and tried unsuccessfully not to listen to the conversation behind her.

"We have to waylay him! He can't know what hit him!"

"Maybe we could do a sneak attack, Heather? Like, we could accidentally break a toilet and he'd have to come fix it. Then we could lock them in the bathroom together and not let them out until he asks her on a date!"

Why had she allowed Miss Daisy to come live with her? She already had enough issues with her gram and Miss Alma and Miss Joyce. She should have known that Miss Daisy would join them in their "matchmaking" attempts, although that sounded more like attempted kidnapping than matchmaking.

"That's brilliant! Now I know why God had you move in with us!"

Move in? Kristen froze. It was true that she had several spare bedrooms in this behemoth of a house, and it was also true that she could use the extra income, since she didn't have a job other than taking care of her gram, but it was not true that she wanted to be ganged up on by four old ladies who had nothing better to do than to try to set her up with any man who breathed and could walk - or crawl - down the sidewalk in front of her house. Last week they had tried to set her up with a man who was sixty if he was a day.

"Guys. Has it ever occurred to any of you that maybe I'm happy being single?"

She knew that line wouldn't work, and of course, it didn't. It only started the conversation about how much better off they were when they were married.

She allowed the chatter to go in one ear and out the other. Really, if she didn't have to watch her gram to make sure she wasn't going to "accidentally" lock Kristen in a bathroom some where, she would be perfectly happy. She lived in the best town in the world, right by the most beautiful lake God created, her gram was in good health and so was she. She had enough money to pay her bills and buy groceries, and really, life was good.

As she flipped the last egg out of the skillet, she thought she heard a knock at the door, but she couldn't be sure with the chatter of the ladies behind her.

Turning the skillet off and moving it off the burner, she left the kitchen without them noticing, and walked to the front door, just to check.

Opening the door she was shocked to see Luke Landry, who could almost be called her nemesis, standing on the porch, one hand in his pocket, one leaning against a big post, his face turned toward the lake like he wanted to be anywhere but there.

"Luke?" she tried not to sound like she hated him. She didn't, of course. It's just that her gram had pushed her toward him so forcefully, that he'd started avoiding her rather obviously, to the point where he physically ran away from her if he saw her, and a girl couldn't help getting a little piqued over something like that.

He startled, and then immediately his eyes flew behind her. "Where's your gram?" he whispered, like he wasn't standing on her porch in broad daylight.

"She's eating a big, strong man for breakfast and you're probably next. Are you sure it's safe to stand this close to me?"

Her words didn't make him relax. More because he was still worried about her gram coming out with a ring and the preacher than he was about getting eaten for breakfast, she was sure, but still.

"Okay, I'll be quick." He was still whispering, and he crept closer, like her gram could hear him taking a normal step. "You know Becky, the little girl with no home?"

"Yeah?" She'd loved her time with Becky, even though it had made her long for a husband and children of her own.

"She's decided who she wants as parents."

Kristen stared at him with her mouth open. She wasn't sure if she was more surprised that Becky got to "choose" her parents, and how did that happen, anyway? Or if she was more surprised that it was Luke who was telling her. Or even that anyone thought she needed told.

"Okay?" she finally said, sounding like she was asking all the questions she couldn't figure out how to ask. "Why are you telling me?"

"Because." He paused, as though gathering up his nerve. "She chose us."

A Gift from Jessie

View this code through your smart phone camera to be taken to a page where you can download a FREE ebook when you sign up to get updates from Jessie Gussman! Find out why people say, "Jessie's is the only newsletter I open and read" and "You make my day brighter. Love, love, love reading your newsletters. I don't know where you find time to write books. You are so busy living life. A true blessing." and "I know from now on that I can't be drinking my morning coffee while reading your newsletter – I laughed so hard I sprayed it out all over the table!"

Claim your free book from Jessie!